The Execution of Mayor Yin
and Other Stories

D0059424

CHINESE LITERATURE IN TRANSLATION

Editors
Irving Yucheng Lo
Joseph S. M. Lau
Leo Ou-fan Lee

The Execution of
MAYOR YIN
and Other Stories
from the
Great Proletarian Cultural
Revolution

CHEN JO-HSI

TRANSLATED FROM THE CHINESE BY
NANCY ING AND HOWARD GOLDBLATT

Indiana University Press   Bloomington

Copyright © 1978 by Chen Jo-hsi

FIRST MIDLAND BOOK EDITION 1979

ALL RIGHTS RESERVED

*No part of this book may be reproduced or utilized in any form
or by any means, electronic or mechanical, including photocopying
and recording, or by any information storage and retrieval system,
without permission in writing from the publisher. The Association
of American University Presses' Resolution on Permissions constitutes
the only exception to this prohibition.*

Manufactured in the United States of America

Library of Congress Cataloging in Publication Data
Chen Jo-hsi
The execution of Mayor Yin.
(Chinese literature in translation)
CONTENTS: The execution of Mayor Yin.—"Chairman Mao
is a rotten egg."—Night duty. [etc.]
I. Title.   II. Series.
PZ4.C5178Ex   [PL2840.J6]   895.1'3'5   78-1956
cl. ISBN 0-253-12475-1   8 9 10 11   89 88
pa. ISBN 0-253-20231-0

For Dr. S. Y. Tuann and the Tuann boys

CONTENTS

Translators' Preface

THE EIGHT STORIES IN THIS COLLECTION WERE PUBLISHED IN
Chinese between November 1974 and August 1976. All but
two were subsequently included in the 1976 anthology *Yin
hsien-chang* (*Mayor Yin*), published in Taipei by the Yüan
Ching Publishing Company. (Technically, *hsien-chang*
means "county magistrate," but since this title is meaningless
in Western countries and is no longer in use in China,
"mayor" has been used in its place.) "Chairman Mao Is a
Rotten Egg" first appeared (under the title "Ching-ching's
Birthday") in the Hong Kong magazine *Ming Pao Monthly*
(No. 122, February 1976), and was later included in the collection of stories *Ch'en Jo-hsi tzu-hsüan chi* (Taipei, 1976).
"Nixon's Press Corps" appeared in the August 5, 1976 edition of the *China Times*.

Four other stories were first published in *Ming Pao
Monthly*: "Mayor Yin" in No. 107, November 1974, "Keng
Erh in Peking" in Nos. 110–12, February–April 1975, "Night
Duty" in No. 116, August 1975, and "The Big Fish" in No.
124, April 1976. Where differences existed between two edi-

tions, the *Ming Pao* version was considered the standard. For
the reader who wishes to compare the translation with the
Chinese originals, a word of caution: a number of changes
have been made by the author, either to correct minor mistakes in the original, to improve the stories' readability and
appeal to the Western reader, or to remove obscure, misleading, or irrelevant references. In most cases these changes
are in the form of deletions, from a few words to a paragraph
or more in English. The author has also Romanized her surname to "Chen" rather than "Ch'en."

This project has been a cooperative venture by the two
translators. The primary division of labor was as follows:
Howard Goldblatt prepared the initial translations of "Keng
Erh in Peking" and "Residency Check," and Nancy Ing
translated the remaining six stories. The editing and preparation of the final manuscript was primarily the responsibility
of Howard Goldblatt.

We would like to acknowledge the assistance of several
people who have made our task easier and more enjoyable
than it might otherwise have been. We are particularly grateful to Professors Joseph S. M. Lau of the University of Wis-
consin and Leo Ou-fan Lee of Indiana University, whose pa-
tience and enthusiasm carried us through the project from
the beginning and whose editing skills have improved the
final product. Our special thanks to Professor Chi-chen
Wang, a pioneer in the translation of Chinese literature, for
his comments and criticisms, and for making available his
own unpublished translation of one of the stories. Thanks
also to Mr. George Cheng of San Francisco State University,
who patiently checked the translation of "Keng Erh in

Peking." We have been fortunate to have the author herself as our foremost critic and advisor, and we are equally fortunate to have our translation prefaced by comments by Simon Leys, the author of *Chinese Shadows*. Finally, we must thank our families, who, because of the sense of urgency that surrounded this project almost from its inception, made many personal sacrifices; without their support and understanding, we could never have completed our task.

N.C.I.

H.G.

San Francisco

Introduction by Simon Leys

Who Is Chen Jo-hsi?

CHEN JO-HSI WAS BORN IN 1938 IN TAIWAN INTO A PROLETAR-
ian family—her father and grandfather were carpenters. Her
importance as a creative writer is already well established on
the Chinese literary scene (outside the People's Republic),
and she is now beginning to receive international recognition.
Her development is interesting. She studied literature at
Taiwan National University and began to publish at a young
age. Her early works, however promising, still betrayed a certain mannerism, their formal research attempting perhaps
to compensate for some lack of substance. During a stay in
the United States, where she was pursuing postgraduate
studies, she and her husband decided to settle in the People's
Republic of China, "to serve the people." As she was soon to
discover, that decision was politically naive; yet the decision
was also incredibly generous and courageous. (That is pre-

cisely what some Maoist sycophants among her overseas compatriots can least forgive her for, since *they* wisely chose to retain the best of both worlds. They enjoy all the perquisites afforded to them by Western universities, and from time to time they make short luxury trips to China, enough to bolster their image and prestige as China experts in the eyes of their foreign audiences.) In 1973, after seven years in China, having lived through the entire "Cultural Revolution," Chen Jo-hsi was lucky enough to be let out of the country with her husband and two children. They first stayed in Hong Kong and then settled in Canada.

Though Chen Jo-hsi was already an active writer when she first entered China, she did not write a single line during all the years she spent there. Once out, however, she was suddenly seized by an overwhelming urge to bear witness in writing to all the people she had left behind—old friends, passing acquaintances, simple men and women who, in their very deprivation, humiliations, and trials, had impressed her with their quiet dignity and irreducible humanity. Perhaps, unconsciously, she was also trying to find the meaning of what had been both the most momentous and the most sterile period of her life, and to come to terms with it; in retrospect, she was attempting to give it sense and value, to make artistic coherence out of its confusion and chaos, to redeem through literature a heartbreaking experiment in human wastefulness. Meanwhile she provides us with a vivid gallery of characters, reflecting different facets of man's condition in today's China, a microcosmic and unforgettable *comédie humaine* of Maoland, complete with its petty cadres, intellectuals, workers, young activists, misfits, faithful believers, shrewd operators, weary old men, social climbers—even Han Suyin herself makes a brief but memorable appearance, which seems only right; that lady, having become utterly fictitious in real life, deserved to retrieve some measure of reality in fiction!

Marginality and Alienation?

The "Great Proletarian Cultural Revolution" was a soul-stirring experience, which directly affected the lives of hundreds of millions of Chinese for fully eleven years.[1] And yet, inside China it has not resulted in a single novel, it has not inspired a single poem, it has not been reflected in a single short story. This paradoxical barrenness of the literary landscape eventually struck Mao himself. With his customary bluntness, he exclaimed in July 1975: "People are afraid to write articles or plays, and we have no novels and no poems."[2] Though the so-called "Gang of Four" is already being conveniently blamed for this dismal situation, there is little likelihood that, under the present leadership, we shall ever see literary descriptions of the glorious battles and victories of the "Cultural Revolution" in print: can you imagine former Red Guards coming back proudly to tell us how they used to kick Teng Hsiao-p'ing around, to bully Ch'en Yi, Chu Teh, and Ho Lung, to drag Lo Jui-ch'ing in front of kangaroo courts and to parade Chou Yang in a dunce cap? Alas, the brave rebels of yesterday are too busy carting manure and planting cabbages in such exotic spots as Sinkiang and Hainan, to find leisure for writing their memoirs.

Since the citizens of the People's Republic are bound to

remain silent on the subject of this momentous era (which they wish they could simply forget), only those writers who managed to leave the country can provide us with a literary reflection of the human condition in China during the eventful decade. A few years ago, a group of young revolutionaries who had escaped to Hong Kong at the risk of their lives put together an interesting and often moving collection of short stories, essays, and poems, some written by themselves, some sent directly from China by friends and comrades left behind. Although revealing and important, this book[3] suffered from a certain artistic immaturity. Ken Ling's autobiographic account of his experiences as a Red Guard leader[4] is *the* basic psychological document on this historical tragedy; yet, strictly speaking, it does not concern us here, since it is not a literary creation, nor was it originally written in Chinese.

Therefore, Chen Jo-hsi remains the only Chinese creative writer of major stature to provide us with literary testimony on the Cultural Revolution era, directly experienced from inside China, at the grass-roots level. Because she has successfully tackled a forbidden reality of such momentous scope, her works have come to occupy a towering position in the middle of an artistic desert; her voice, which she deliberately keeps subdued and plain, the better to convey the overwhelming emotional intensity of her message, acquires a unique resonance for being surrounded by a massive silence. Thus, there would seem to be no need to underline further the central relevance of her writings to Chinese contemporary reality—and yet, when I spoke on this topic at a conference on Literature and Contemporary Asian Societies, I had the interesting surprise of seeing it listed on the program under the label of "marginality and alienation." Still, I can somehow see the convener's point. Let us examine it, for it might help us better to define Chen's position in the context of Chinese contemporary literature.

Consider the question from the other side: what kind of literature is it that is neither alienated nor marginal in today's China? The answer is, of course: any piece of writing that has successfully cleared the various hurdles of censorship; docilely met the numerous, intricate, and ever-changing demands of political orthodoxy; and thus been found fit to appear in print. Second question: can such writings, non-marginal and non-alienated as they are, still be considered literature? What is literature? (For some fellow Sinologists, bent on doing a *scientific* study of literature and ever wary of committing the sin of *subjective* value judgments, the sole fact that "it" has appeared in print seems a sufficient criterion; I always wonder why they do not include the telephone directory in their sphere of scholarly inquiry.) Let us look for a moment at the requirements writers had to fulfill under Madame Mao's cultural rule: I have already quoted elsewhere, in full, the typical and very precise list of conditions set by a Maoist literary journal for potential contributors.[5] These specifications, which have actually directed and controlled all literary activity in China for the past eleven years (and are still controlling it today to a large extent), may appear grotesque; nevertheless, let us not forget that they also represent a remarkable attempt at actually enforcing in the most literal, concrete, and complete way, the cultural policy first formulated by Mao himself in his celebrated intervention at the 1942 Yenan forum on literature and art.

(In this matter, as in any other, the "Gang of Four," which would be better named "Gang of Five," since without Mao it could never have come into existence, represents simply a brand of undiluted Maoism, which eventually had to be declared unfit for human consumption because of its very degree of purity.)

The kind of writing that such guidelines foster was (thirty years in advance!) aptly qualified by Lu Hsün—the great revolutionary writer whom everyone in China praises and no one reads: "To my mind, any kind of literature that can be used for the goal of political propaganda is devoid of persuasive force. Good literature always refuses to be ordered from outside, it never cares about practical considerations, it spontaneously springs from the heart. If you set a topic for writers to compose on, how does that differ from having them writing eight-legged[6] essays? Not only will it be worthless as literature, but worse, it will fail to move people."[7]

Without doubt, the eight-legged essay must be the epitome of non-marginal non-alienated writing: officially sponsored by the government, it was the key to social status, bureaucratic recognition, and political power. Are eight-legged essays literature?

The great paradox of these non-alienated non-marginal eight-legged essays, which in the People's Republic now pass for literature, is that they are totally alienated from the people, with whom they bear only coincidental relation. They are not supposed to describe "ordinary characters" (*chung-chien jen-wu*) but only "heroic stereotypes" (*ying-hsiung tien-hsing*) and are utterly marginal to life, which they do not dare reflect too closely since it would be slanderous to "our great socialist motherland."[8] The very esthetic policies of the Party prevent them from revealing anything of the actual human, social, economic, and political conditions. They do not mirror reality, but only what the Leadership decided reality should be like; they are not descriptive, but pedagogic and normative; they do not draw their inspiration from nature, self, and society, but from the memos and instructions issued by the bureaucrats of the Propaganda Department.

The corollary of such a situation is that genuine literature must, by definition, be created by social outcasts and political exiles, misfits who remain marginal to officialdom and alienated from the state. In striving to retain their artistic integrity, writers condemn themselves to becoming heretics.

There is a much broader truth to this phenomenon, which expresses itself in all aspects of intellectual and spiritual activity, and could be called "the creative function of the exile." Claude Roy described it well: "To achieve a clear view implies initially a certain distance, and nearly always eventuates in exile—not necessarily exile from a place, from a motherland, but always from power, wealth and authority. I do not believe that it is by chance that, of the seven men who really enlightened the human mind in the last hundred years, there were five Jews, one Irishman, one Catalan— seven 'dagoes,' and all of them exiles: Marx, Freud, Kafka, Einstein, Wittgenstein, James Joyce and Picasso. In order to see clearly, one must look from a certain distance, but he who sees too clearly ends up being hated by the shortsighted and the blind."[9] A study of the contribution of the exile to the cultural and intellectual life of our age still remains to be done. (How much poorer, for instance, would be our understanding of politics without the illuminating lessons given us by the great Soviet dissenters—Chafarevitch, Zinoviev, Orlov, Solzhenitsyn, Amalrik, etc. And more is to come, since in this field the Chinese are now only beginning to make themselves heard.)

It is striking to note that, since antiquity, one important tradition of Chinese literary criticism assigned a privileged function to the exile, the marginal person, the alienated writer; literature was viewed as a lone dissent (the works of the ancient poet Ch'ü Yuan), as a venting of moral indignation, frustration, and wrath (the writings of the historian Ssu-ma Ch'ien). These notions, constantly revived from age to age, acquired a renewed vitality in the twentieth century. Chou Tso-jen, for instance, saw literature as essentially "rebellious,"[10] while Lu Hsün, in his essay on the "Divergent Paths of Literature and Politics,"[11] gave the most articulate and forceful expression to this concept of the writer's *permanent alienation* from political authority. According to him, the writer should be a constant thorn in the flesh of the ruling Establishment: "The statesman hates the writer because the writer sows seeds of dissent; what the statesman dreams of is to be able to prevent people from thinking, and thus he always accuses the artists and writers of upsetting his orderly state."

In order to "upset the orderly state today," Chinese writers do not need to be fighters challenging the government; it is enough that, faithful to their calling, they simply endeavor to bear a sober testimony to the condition of their people. If such a pursuit has reduced Chen Jo-hsi to a state of "marginality and alienation" and eventually drove her into exile, that means that she has come to occupy her rightful place in one of China's longest living literary traditions—the one that is currently of most burning relevance.

Literature and Politics

The possibility of "alienated and marginal" writers such as Chen working clandestinely inside China today is not entirely precluded (witness some of the pieces in *Daring to Sing a Song which Moves the Earth*, see p.xv and n.3, or even powerful manifestoes written by political dissidents such as Li Yi-che). Still, it is drastically limited, first because such activity is repressed with penalties too terrifying to bear contemplating, and second because the entire sociopolitical fabric of life is tightly woven in a way that leaves no room for such pursuit, either in terms of material leisure and privacy, or in terms of psychological and spiritual autonomy. (In this respect, compared with the Russians, the Chinese pay a heavy price for being more cultured; even in its harshest periods, the Soviet system remained full of loopholes, owing to its crude background and native inefficiency, while the Maoist regime, benefitting from the sophistication and the organizational genius of the Chinese people, was able to outpace its Stalinist prototype by far.)

As I mentioned above, all the while that Chen Jo-hsi lived in the People's Republic she did no writing, and she even came to believe that she would never write again. In a way, the sudden and total paralysis that struck her pen in China is as revealing as the creative flow that began pouring from it after she left. Her experience should help us to understand why, after "Liberation," all the leading figures of modern Chinese literature fell into almost total silence and sterility: Pa Chin, Mao Tun, Lao She, Chang T'ien-yi, Ch'ien Chung-shu, Shen Ts'ung-wen, etc., either produced only a few trite *pièces de circonstance*, or buried themselves in scholarly research. None of them succeeded in adding even one significant creation to his earlier works. There are more implications to this than mere cultural bankruptcy. As Michel Tournier observed: "Tyranny is the most ruinous of all luxuries. It is true at all levels, and in a country where poets are silenced or exiled, it is fatal that housewives must queue in front of the shops."[12]

Since the silence of Chinese writers is so heavily loaded with political meaning, when one of them recovers his or her voice, the message must inescapably present a political dimension. Primarily this is brought about by the system itself, rather than being inherent in the writer's work. As J.-F. Revel pointed out: "It is not because a book 'hides' a political intention that totalitarianism condemns it. On the contrary, it is because the regime is totalitarian that any book always presents for it a political dimension; more exactly, it can *only* have a political dimension against, or in favor of, this regime, since the regime is conceived as a single block whose elements cannot be dissociated."[13]

In the empire of lies, the humblest truth is revolutionary, mere reality is subversive. And so it happens that Chen Jo-hsi's short stories, which sometimes concern themselves only with small happenings in the everyday life of ordinary people, subtly painted in Chekhovian shades of grey, acquire

in the eyes of their Maoist critics the fierce appearance of a
machine de guerre!

Nor did the political potential of Chen's stories escape
the attention of the Taiwan authorities. Actually, the first
impulse of the censors was to ban their publication. Didn't
they show citizens of the People's Republic buying chicken
at the market, eating mutton in the restaurants, when according to the orthodox Kuomintang propaganda, they should
have been munching the bark of trees? Worse, there were
references to the popularity enjoyed by Chou En-lai among
the masses, and even the unforgettable portrait of an attractive girl, proud daughter of the New China, happy and
confident, who embarked enthusiastically in Mao's Cultural Revolution. All this must be the work of an agent of
the United Front! However, later on, shrewder officials re-
versed this initial judgment and decided that, on the contrary, it would be better to make maximum use of Chen's
writings, with a few little cuts here and there, for anti-
Communist propaganda purposes.[14] This decision was in a
way as unfortunate as the earlier one, since it equally mis-
understood Chen's significance.

That Chen's stories do have a political content cannot be
denied. We can already foresee the doctoral theses that will
be validly written on "aspects of Chinese sociopolitical culture, as reflected in Chen Jo-hsi's fiction"; and, indeed, by
reading a few of her works, one can obtain a deeper and fuller
understanding of what Maoism in action is really like than
by perusing an entire political science library. (How many
times have Chinese friends—former citizens of the People's
Republic who were despairing that they would ever be able

to make a Western audience really grasp what they were trying to convey about China—pressed for quick translations of Chen's works, which alone, they feel, could bridge that communication gap?) And yet, even though Chen's writings do have a purpose and a motivation, it should be emphasized that they are literary and not political.

Chen Jo-hsi writes fiction, not essays. In a theoretical essay, a writer endeavors to convey ideas already clearly formed in his or her mind, while fiction is creation; fiction writing is an experience in discovery for the author. An essay is two-dimensional and develops on a mere intellectual plane; in fiction, on the other hand, the eruption of life and reality adds a third dimension: unpredictable, inexhaustible, indefinable, ambiguous, multifaced, contradictory, forever escaping the narrow certainty of definitions and conclusions.

When an essay affords two or three different interpretations, that is an indication that either the author or the reader is at fault: the point has not been properly made or grasped. On the contrary, when a novel lends itself to different readings, it has fully succeeded as a creation: it partakes in the reality of life, which is never univocal.

Writers or scholars for whom the People's Republic of China remains a mere intellectual issue, either because they lack personal and emotional involvement in it or because they have been deprived of deeper human contacts with it (as is generally the sad lot of foreign residents, who are strictly segregated from the Chinese people), may find it easy enough to write theoretical essays on this subject—be they objective (whatever that word might mean), critical, or eulogistic. But for one who has really *lived* there as a Chinese among Chinese, who has been absorbed, sucked into the maelstrom of reality, who by turns has been sustained and bruised by the dense network of Chinese human relationship—subtle, all-pervasive, warm and cruel, supple and ruthless, bitter and funny, odious and lovable, and always overwhelming—judgments are not easy to pass, and conclusions not lightly drawn. For a writer shaken by an experience to the very roots of his or her self and left confused and wounded, on the edge of a new discovery, of a new intuition of the world and of one's place in it, fiction writing becomes a uniquely effective response.

It was the first move of the Taiwan censors that was the "right" one: from their point of view, Chen's books would indeed be dangerous, inasmuch as they reveal that the human facts of the People's Republic are complex and irreducible to any propaganda clichés (in their hostility toward novelists' ambiguities, Kuomintang censors are the equal of their Peking colleagues in being suspicious of everyday truths and actively discourage writers from depicting reality).

If fiction is the best tool for exploring a perplexing and manifold experience, the very laws of the craft prevent the writer from falsifying that experience and from imposing any prefabricated conceptions upon the reader, under the penalty of automatically killing the writer's own creation. Here, artistic achievement is the reward for, and the guarantee of, intellectual integrity.

With a sharply and clearly conceived thesis to demonstrate, with a strong and lucid political motivation, one can write a splendid essay, but never a true novel.[15] If the novelist loads the dice the better to make a point—indeed, if he or she merely has a point to make!—the fiction immediately sinks under the weight of the writer's conscious purpose, and the characters turn into puppets. The puppeteer leads the wooden marionettes, but the novelist is led by the living creatures. (Remember Dostoyevsky hurrying back to his writing table, in his impatience to learn what would be Rogojin's next move!) Even though there have been great novelists who thought that they had a doctrine to teach, if they achieved greatness it is only because they forgot all about it in the process of writing and let themselves be carried away by their creation. Balzac held preposterous social theories, which did not prevent Marx from finding constant inspiration in reading his novels, since the writer's creative genius had caught the social reality of his age in all its living complexity. It is only in this same sense that Chen's stories present a political content; to assign a political purpose to them would not only be misleading, it would also be tantamount to ignoring their very nature and achievement as literary creations.

To say that Chen has no political purpose does not mean that her writing is without motivation. On the contrary, what makes her stories so compelling is precisely the fact that they were written under such an intense inner compulsion. During the first part of her career, in Taiwan and in America, Chen shared the fate of so many gifted young writers for whom their very talent is a curse: they are (to borrow the Chinese saying) "heroes without a field wherein to display their valor." There is in them an urge to write, and yet they have essentially nothing to say. This sad condition is at the origin of countless distinguished, sometimes even stylistically brilliant, pieces of writing, whose only defect—unredeemable—is that they are perfectly superfluous. Seldom does an experience of compelling urgency come to be entrusted to an eager and ready talent! For such an encounter to happen, no hardship would be too high a price to pay: to be blessed at last with this certainty, to feel one's pen invested with an authority that immensely exceeds the scope of one's petty self!

Thus, for Chen, there is now this load of living reality that possesses her and presses to be delivered, this crowd of characters in her memory, countless faces jostling and crying to be heard, who will leave her no rest until they all get written down. The formal and technical problems that used to hold most of her attention when she had little to express have all vanished. While insignificant artists write as they *wish* (hence the flowery ornaments, the purple prose, the gratuitous stylistic experiments), she is now a true writer: she writes *as she can*, as if under dictation, she is driven by an inner necessity that leaves her no choice but to bear witness to life and reality—our only masters.

NOTES

1. I adopt here the chronology of Hua Kuo-feng: ". . . our first Great Proletarian Cultural Revolution which lasted eleven years . . ." (*Political Report to the 11th Party Congress*, August 1977).

2. Quoted by Hua Kuo-feng, ibid.

3. *Kan yu ke yin tung ti ai* ("Daring to Sing a Song which Moves the Earth") (Hong Kong: Ch'i-shih nien-tai, 1974).

4. Ken Ling, *The Revenge of Heaven* (New York: Putnam, 1972).

5. "Our publication welcomes all manuscripts which fulfill the following conditions:

"A. All novels, essays, articles, works of art which present in a healthy way a revolutionary content. They must: (1) exalt with deep and warm proletarian feelings the great Chairman Mao; exalt the great, glorious and infallible Chinese Communist Party; exalt the great victory of the proletarian revolutionary line of Chairman Mao; (2) following the examples of the Revolutionary Model operas, strive with zeal to create peasant and worker heroes; (3) on the theme of the struggle between the two lines, reflect the people's revolutionary struggle, which has lasted for half a century under the leadership of our Party, and, especially, the unbroken revolutionary struggle fought under the aegis of the dictatorship of the proletariat; reflect the unanimous struggle of the population of our province [Kwangtung, in this case] following the direction given by Chairman Mao, and the unfolding of that struggle in its victorious progression.

"B. In artistic and literary theory: we welcome texts that have a mass, revolutionary, and militant character, advocate a simple language and clear lessons, have a lively, vigorous, and original style; we welcome short popularizing essays, with a strong and persuasive force in ideas and analysis on such themes as the study of literary and artistic theories in Marxism–Leninism, the living understanding of the artistic and literary Thought of Mao Tse-tung, the living understanding of the creative experience in the study of the Revolutionary Model operas; we welcome articles that, taking Marxism–Leninism as a guide, study the problems of socialist and artistic literary creation, deepen the denunciation of anti-Marxist points of view and of the revisionist black line in the artistic and literary field, points of view propagated by Liu Shao-ch'i-type swindlers" (*Kwangtung wen-yi*, No. 1, 1973).

6. The notorious stultified form of literary composition, which was compulsory in the civil service examinations of the old empire.

7. "Ke-ming shih-tai ti wen-hsueh" ("Literature of a Revolutionary Period"), in *Ehr yi chi, Lu Hsun ch'üan-chi* ("Complete Works of Lu Hsun") (Peking 1963), Vol. III, p. 313.

8. Most significant in this respect, beginning in the late fifties and culminating with the Cultural Revolution, were the veering away from the precepts of "socialist realism," which has now become

a Trojan horse introducing reality into the citadel of Maoist esthetics, and their replacement with "revolutionary romanticism," a dogma better insulated against the real world.

9. Claude Roy, *Somme toute* (Paris: Gallimard, 1976), p. 276.

10. Chou Tso-jen, "Yen chih ts'ao pa," in *Yung jih chi*, p. 181.

11. "Wen-yi yü cheng-chih ti ch'i-t'u," in *Chi wai chi, Lu Hsun ch'üan-chi* (Peking 1963), VII, pp. 103-10.

12. *Le vent Paraclet* (Paris: Gallimard, 1977), p. 142.

13. *La tentation totalitaire* (Paris: Laffont, 1976), p. 61.

14. Most of the stories in the present collection appeared originally in *Ming Pao Monthly* (Hong Kong) and were later published with minor alterations (some imposed by political censorship in Taiwan) in one volume, *Yin hsien-chang* (Taipei: Yuan-ching, 1976).

15. *Nineteen Eighty Four*, for instance, is a masterpiece of the essay; no one would ever mistake it for a genuine novel. The *concept* of Big Brother has been effectively driven into our minds, but we hardly remember the characters—let alone the names—of Winston and Julia. The same applies for most of Malraux, Koestler, etc. Conversely, just as there are essays disguised as novels, there are also novels disguised as essays (especially in the area of historical and biographical writing).

The Execution of Mayor Yin
and Other Stories

The Execution of
Mayor Yin

MAYOR YIN AND I MET ONLY TWICE, BUT I SHALL NEVER FOR-
get him.

In the fall of 1966 I went to Sian from Peking and stayed
at the home of my friend, Lao Wu.* His only son, Hsiao
Wu,† was one of those arrogant Red Guards who, despite the
fact that he was only a second-year high school student, ex-
hibited an air of authority, loudly proclaiming such revolutionary slogans as "Support Chairman Mao" and "Rebellion
is right and just."

He could not bear to take off his olive-green uniform
long enough for it to be laundered, so his collar and cuffs
were always shiny with oily grime. But his red armband was
bright and clean, and whenever he met anyone he would

---

*Lao (literally "old") is used with a person's surname as an expression
of familiarity or friendship.
†Hsiao (literally "little") serves the same function as Lao.

stand with his right hand on his hip, forcing people to recognize the authority that five-inch-wide band of dazzling red
silk represented. He and another Red Guard were preparing
to set off for Hsingan County in southern Shensi province
to kindle the fire of rebellion there. The spirit of revolution
lagged in that backward area, which did not even have a Red
Guard organization, so Sian's Red Guard Headquarters decided to send two competent cadremen to set up operations.

Hsiao Wu volunteered for the job. He was originally
from Hsingan and had moved to the provincial capital with
his parents when he was twelve years old. He could thus serve
the revolution and also revisit his old home and see his
friends and relatives. Both private and public interests could
be served. Of course, it was taboo to speak of "serving private
and public interests," since that was the time of the slogan
"Down with private interests; serve only the public good."
This sort of thing simply invited criticism. One had to base
all personal conduct on Mao Tse-tung's teachings: "Never
think of yourself; think only of others."

It happened that I had just completed my official mission and did not have to report back to Peking for almost
two weeks. On a former assignment I had visited all the
famous scenic spots of Sian, such as the Great and Small
Wild Geese Pagodas, the Forest of Monuments, and the ar-
tifacts from the diggings of Panpienpo. Since I had nothing
better to do around there, I accepted Lao Wu's suggestion
that I accompany his son and a schoolmate to southern
Shensi and take in the sights of the Hanchung Basin.

It took us a day and a night by bus to cross the peaks of
the Chinling Mountains and reach Hsingan. All along the

way it was mountain after mountain, and the bus was forever tilting to one side. I was constantly dizzy and a little
nauseated, and even when I got off at the station I felt that
I was leaning as I walked. The Chinling Mountains are like
a massive screen, and the scenery changed completely from
the northern to the southern slopes. When we left Sian it
was already late autumn, and the trees were bare, the grass
a withered brown; but in Hsingan the land was green as far
as the eye could see, as if one had found oneself south of the
Yangtze River.

Hsiao Wu arranged for me to stay at the home of his
relative, Lao Yin, while he and his schoolmate went to stay
at the county middle school dormitory. Lao Yin was past
seventy, but he was still strong and hearty. His wife had
just died the year before, so he lived all alone in a large one-
room brick house, which he kept meticulously neat and
clean. He seemed genuinely happy to accommodate guests
from afar. As soon as we stepped inside the door he cheerfully put aside his long pipe, rolled up his sleeves, and began
to cook. Hsiao Wu and his friend, in the tradition of the
Liberation Army, laid down their packs and started to chop
firewood and carry water from the well.

After dinner, just as Hsiao Wu and his friend were about
to leave for the dormitory, a bespectacled man in a cadre
uniform strode into the room. When Hsiao Wu saw him
he hesitated a moment before reluctantly addressing him as
Uncle. Then he introduced us, saying, "This is a distant
uncle of mine," stressing the word "distant."

We did not know the visitor's name, so both Hsiao Wu's
schoolmate and I very politely followed suit in addressing

him as Uncle. As soon as he finished with the introductions, Hsiao Wu hurriedly grabbed my hand to look at my wrist-watch. "It's late," he exclaimed. "I'm afraid the students' dormitory will close." In obvious haste, he urged his friend to get ready, then picked up his pack and left with him.

This uncle of Hsiao Wu's seemed surprised and non-plussed by their sudden departure. While greeting us warmly his eyes continued to gaze with wonder at Hsiao Wu's red armband. He was a very tall man, dark and thin, about fifty years old. His back was straight and strong, suggesting that he must have presented an impressive figure in his youth. He looked you straight in the eye, and when he listened he would bend his head slightly as if he were afraid to miss a single word. The expression on his face was diffident and gentle. He wore a neat gray Chung-shan suit,* cotton socks and shoes, showing him to be a typical old cadreman from any part of China, north or south.

He sat down, and after exchanging amenities with Lao Yin, turned and asked me courteously who I was. Upon hearing that I was on a sightseeing visit to southern Shensi, he seemed more relaxed and expressed his welcome. He spoke with the sincere diffidence of the midlander. "Our Hsingan is a backward, out-of-the-way place. Aside from this boundless chain of Chinling Mountains and Ta-pa Moun-tain, there's only the Han River. However, in the mountains to the north there are some waterfalls that are worth seeing. It's too bad that at the moment we are again involved with

---

*Chung-shan chuang is the high-collared attire worn throughout China. The top is also referred to as a Mao jacket.

a campaign that makes it impossible for me to get away, or I'd be happy to escort you there."

Maybe the word "campaign" reminded him of something, for his face darkened and he sighed softly. Lao Yin turned on the room's single light bulb and brought him a cup of hot water, but he didn't drink it. He just sat for a while in silence, then got up and left.

The next day hospitable Lao Yin got up early in the morning to cook some rice porridge, breaking his habit of many years of eating only two meals a day. I was much refreshed after a good night's sleep and suddenly remembered the cured pork and dried beef I had bought in Sian. I hastened to offer them to Lao Yin. As we ate our porridge I mentioned "Uncle" and learned that he was the mayor of Hsingan. His surname was also Yin, and thus he was a kinsman of Lao Yin.

"He was commended for his meritorious service during the Revolution and became the acting mayor. After Liberation he continued to serve as a member of the district committee, but everyone continued to address him as Mayor Yin," said Lao Yin.

It turned out that Mayor Yin had been an officer under the Kuomintang general Hu Tsung-nan, and with thousands of soldiers under his command, he had guarded a strategic pass along the southeastern edge of the Chinling Mountains. Since it would have been almost impossible to take the pass by force, underground Communist agents had been sent to work on subverting Colonel Yin's loyalty. At the time he was a young man in his twenties who commanded the allegiance of his soldiers, men recruited from the area around the Chinling Mountains, so when he had resolutely thrown down his arms and gone over to the Communists, his troops followed him.

"And so, without wasting a single bullet, the red flag began to fly over three counties in southern Shensi."

As he finished talking Lao Yin lit his long pipe and took several vigorous puffs on it, blowing out the smoke slowly. His old eyes twinkled, as if the memories of the past could still stir his emotions. Since I have always respected those who could see a situation clearly, discerning what is right from what is wrong, I too applauded Mayor Yin's wisdom.

"I'm not trying to paint a flattering picture of him just because he's a kinsman of mine—you can ask anyone who lives within forty li* of here. When he went over to the other side he wasn't seeking personal wealth or position; he only asked for a guarantee of safety for his soldiers, and that they be given the chance to reform and make a new start. I don't think there are many Kuomintang officers who could behave like that!"

"There certainly aren't many like that," I agreed.

"Nowadays it's those who come from a good background who have the advantage. During the land reform period the working committee in his village classified his old mother as a poor peasant. But he actually requested that her status be changed, since when his father was alive they had often hired laborers to help out at the busiest times on the farm, and according to government policy, that would classify

---

*One li is approximately one-third of a mile.

them as rich peasants. In the end they put her down as a middle peasant."

"Well, that shows that Mayor Yin was pretty radical!"

"Hm, you don't know the half of it. During the 1951 Three Antis and Five Antis campaigns* he was the only cadreman in the county who came out unscathed. Even the Party Committee secretary was changed several times. As I recall, it was during those campaigns that the first one was dismissed for being corrupt."

"How could they change the secretary of the Party Committee so many times?" I was somewhat taken aback by this remark.

"Ai, the situation in our county is rather complicated, mainly because the peasants could not keep up with the constant political changes in politics. So production also suffered. When the rate of production failed to increase, other problems developed, and since these problems could not be solved, they got rid of the secretary. To tell the truth, ever since Liberation, production has improved and our lives got a little better, though we still cannot compare with that of the people in the midlands. You've just come from there and you know that in those eight hundred *li* along the Ch'in River the harvest from one season can last for two years. The situation isn't bad here, but it's much worse in the smaller areas. Whenever there are periods of bad weather,

---

*The Three Antis campaign (*san-fan yün-tung*) was directed against corruption, waste, and bureaucratism; the Five Antis campaign (*wu-fan yün-tung*) was aimed at bribery, evasion of taxes, theft of state property, skimping on work and cheating on materials, and theft of state economic information.

famine still occurs and people must chew leaves and grass and the bark of trees. A few years back during a bad harvest I went to my old home in the mountains. My neighbor's daughter could not come out to greet me, for she had no trousers to wear. Her mother had exchanged their cloth coupon for food. This is just between you and me, and I trust you won't turn around and brand me a counterrevolutionary."

I shook my head solemnly. "I'm not a Party member, and besides, I detest those who report on people behind their backs."

Lao Yin spat contemptuously, expressing his agreement.

"There were plenty of hardships here during those three years. But in all fairness, I've lived more than seventy years, and I've seen worse times than these before Liberation. In those days people not only sold their children, there were even cases of cannibalism. During the recent period of bad times, the cadres were just as hungry as everyone else, so the people were placated by firing the Party secretary. The Communists acknowledge their mistakes, and for that I respect them. And in a way it's fortunate that these three years have been so difficult, or else Mayor Yin would've fallen long ago."

"Why, did he do something wrong?"

"He spoke out a few times during the Hundred Flowers period,* and in fact he led the criticism of the agricultural

---

*A campaign for freer criticism of the cadres and bureaucracy begun in 1956 under the slogan "Let a hundred flowers bloom together, let the hundred schools of thought contend." The outpouring of criticism by intellectuals led to an anti-rightist campaign intended to stifle all criticism.

policies. Who would have guessed that there would suddenly be an anti-rightist campaign and that he would almost get a rightist label hung on him? His wife, who'd been working in the county, was transferred, and if it hadn't been for Mayor Yin's meritorious service, she would've been sent to the caves in northern Shensi. They had plans to make him a Party member and he'd already made application, but this anti-rightist campaign spoiled everything. Actually, he never wanted to become a Party member anyway. He once told me that never in his life would he be able to master the theories of Marxism.

"After the campaign was launched it was rumored that he would be stripped of his committee membership and dismissed from his position as mayor. But in the spring and summer of 1960 we were plagued with the worst drought we'd ever had, and not a single kernel of corn or wheat was harvested. The peasants' morale was very low, and there were many grain robberies. Even the grain sent by the government for famine relief couldn't solve the problem. So they were not only unable to dismiss Mayor Yin, they had to delegate to him the responsibility for handling agricultural production. During those two years he personally went into the villages and called on the peasants to keep up production. At the same time he relaxed regulations and encouraged the peasants to exert themselves to the utmost. He allowed them to retain small plots of land for private use and permitted them a little more freedom in order to stimulate self-interest and establish a common market for free trade . . . "

"Aiya, Uncle Yin," I couldn't keep from interrupting him, "there you go, bringing up that Three Freedoms and

One Contract affair!* You should know that the aim of the Cultural Revolution is to discover who was responsible for that fiasco. The wall posters in Peking are already hinting at Liu Shao-ch'i, without mentioning names, and urging that this restoration of imperialist policies be soundly criticized!"

"Is that true?" The old man stared at me.

"Of course it's true!" I lowered my voice. "I heard many people saying so with my own ears."

"I'm getting so old I can't keep up with things." As he shook his head in discouragement the few white hairs on his forehead quivered. Suddenly his attitude hardened again and he knitted his brow so tightly that his face looked like a withered orange. "I don't understand," he said angrily. "Wouldn't the peasants have revolted if he hadn't done what he did?"

"Don't talk like that!" I warned him hastily. "If your relative did carry out this policy, then he won't be able to escape being criticized and condemned."

The old man began to laugh, saying with a careless shrug: "So what? Public criticism is common fare for the cadres, and even little fry like me have been publicly criticized countless times over the past few years."

"You're right. They say that this time the purpose is to oppose and guard against revisionism. Our main task is to dig up the roots of Liu Shao-ch'i's revisionist policies. As to

---

*(San-tzu i-pao.) The Three Freedoms were extension of plots of land for private production, free markets, and increase of private enterprise. The One Contract was a contracted obligation by each household for producing a fixed quantity of grain.

the people who merely carried out his policies, they will only undergo thought reform."

"That's as it should be," the old man agreed, somewhat mollified. "When Mayor Yin was pushing that Three Freedoms and One Contract way of thinking he was only following orders from above. How could he have invented something like that himself? Ever since the anti-rightist campaign he has been County Committee chairman in name only."

Although his mind seemed clear on the matter now, Lao Yin became preoccupied, remaining silent and thoughtful. When he was not busy he would sit on a small stool in the doorway smoking his long pipe, his eyes blinking nervously as though he were troubled.

Things really moved fast after that. In the two days since I last saw Hsiao Wu, large red and green posters had already appeared in the small county town, announcing the establishment of a local Red Guard organization. They called on all citizens and students to rise up and join in the revolution, pointedly urging all political cadremen to purify themselves by fire and carry out their revolutionary duties voluntarily.

The main thoroughfare of the town was the east–west highway. Lao Yin's house was at the west end, and standing on tiptoe by the side of the road looking eastward, I could see all the most important buildings in town: the county high school, the elementary school, and the movie theater at the farthest end; the County Committee office, the department store, and the bus station in the middle; and the county hospital near the west end. During those few days I often saw middle school students with brushes and pails full of paste, which they smeared on the walls with bold strokes before sticking up the large posters. Peasants going into town on business stood around watching curiously, the younger ones even pointing as they exchanged comments. Occasionally the people's attention was captured by the noise of a motor, as a small tractor would come down from the mountains, filled with many enthusiastic, windblown faces. As soon as they had passed, everyone's eyes would turn back to the huge black letters and the rousing slogans of the posters:

DRAG OUT THE CAPITALIST ROADER X X X !
WE SHALL FIGHT ANYONE WHO TRIES TO COVER UP!
X X X MUST BOW DOWN AND CONFESS HIS GUILT!
X X, YOUR CRIMES HAVE BEEN FOUND OUT. YOUR
DAYS ARE NUMBERED!
SHENSI RED COMMAND AND HSINGAN REVOLUTIONARY
GROUP, MARCH FORWARD COURAGEOUSLY!

On the streets people could be heard loudly discussing the accusations against the Party secretary. The Red Guards wanted to hold a big meeting to criticize and denounce him for resisting the Sixteen Points,* for sabotaging the campaign, and for corruption. They even threatened to parade him through the streets! Then just as the campaign reached its peak, a large new poster suddenly appeared on the main gate of the county elementary school denouncing another

---

*The sixteen points (*shih-liu t'iao*) adopted by the eleventh plenum of the Central Committee of the Chinese Communist Party on August 8, 1966 for the purpose of regulating the activities of the Red Guard.

cadreman. I walked over to take a look at it, but the crowd was three or four deep, so it took me some time to work my way up to the poster.

The heading read: "WHO IS THE REAL CLASS ENEMY?" Beneath it was a smaller caption: "Beware of Catching the Small Shrimps and Letting the Big Fish Slip Away!" It urged the people to drag out the real class enemy from the County Committee, the underworld criminal, the warlord of the Kuomintang era. It stated that he had masqueraded as a radical, lied about his background, and habitually fleeced the people, and that his landlord-class wife had resisted any and all kinds of reformation, and so on. At first I didn't know whom this referred to, but when I heard the people around me discussing the matter, it was clear that it was aimed at Mayor Yin. The flames had finally reached his head. Although I realized that the situation was inevitable and was dictated by the course of events, I heaved a sigh nonetheless.

After dinner that evening Hsiao Wu came to see me, bringing a bus ticket to Hanchung for the next day. I mentioned the poster I had seen that day and casually asked him what the problem was with his "Mayor Uncle."

On hearing the word "Uncle" his face turned bright red, and his nostrils twitched with indignation. He began to grumble about the difficulties of organizing work, complaining that the mountain youths were backward and stubborn and had no understanding whatsoever of policies. The newly organized revolutionary corps, it turned out, had been manipulated by someone in the background who, without warning, called for first purging the mayor and then arresting the Party secretary.

"This must be the work of Liu Shao-ch'i's running dogs," Hsiao Wu said as he ground his teeth. "They want to protect those heading down the capitalist road, so they've changed the direction of the campaign and begun striking an already dying dog."

"Why? Is your uncle a veteran of political campaigns?" I quizzed Hsiao Wu.

He shrugged his shoulders. "At most he is only a rightist who has slipped through the net. My uncle . . . "

At this point he stopped abruptly and shook his head vigorously, as though he had made up his mind to disavow the family relationship.

"Everyone knows that Yin Fei-lung has been the mayor in name only these many years. To go after him with all this fanfare is straying far from the main path. This is nothing short of catching the small shrimp and letting the big fish slip away. That Party secretary is rotten and corrupt, and he behaves immorally with women. The people were really angered, yet they let him go so easily. I suspect he's the one in the background who is manipulating some of the Red Guards and creating this split. But when I suggested that we go after the real culprit, there were some who accused me of trying to shield my own relative. Their mothers'. . . !"

He grew angrier as he talked, so full of resentment that he could not sit still on the bench. Suddenly he stood up and pounded his fist on the dining table, almost breaking the dishes. I was startled and did not know how to comfort him. I glanced at Lao Yin. He blinked his eyes indifferently as he smoked his long pipe. Occasionally he would look coldly at Hsiao Wu without saying a word.

As soon as the sun set behind the mountain, the wind began to rise. It became stronger and louder. Afraid of being caught in a storm, Hsiao Wu refused to stay any longer; he turned up his collar and hurried off. Lao Yin turned on the light and cleared the dining table. He boiled some water and then banked the fire, while I packed a bag for the next day's trip.

By the time we finished washing up it was nine-thirty, a time when most people in this mountain city had already retired. Just as we were about to turn out the light and get into bed, there was a very soft knock on the door. Lao Yin was sitting on the edge of the bed, bending over to take off his shoes, and apparently hadn't heard it. Wondering who it could be, I unbolted the door. A figure slipped in with the wind, and quickly closed the door behind him. In the light of the swaying lamp I could see that it was Mayor Yin. His coming to call at this late hour took me completely by surprise.

He apologized for disturbing us. "It isn't often that I have a chance to meet a comrade from Peking, so I couldn't refrain from asking you a few questions."

I invited him to sit at the table. Lao Yin pulled his shoes on and came over to join us. Mayor Yin removed his cap and glasses; and probably because he did not know where to begin, he took out his handkerchief and concentrated on polishing his glasses. His bronzed face, appearing larger than usual without his glasses, was overshadowed with fatigue and uncertainty. We were sitting very close to one another, and I noticed a scar under the corner of his left eye that stretched across to his ear. There was also an inch-long surgical scar on the back of his right hand. I surmised that they stemmed from his days as a soldier. Except for these marks, it would be impossible to imagine him now as the "warlord" the large posters accused him of being. I didn't know whether he was aware that his name had been posted, and I couldn't bring myself to ask him.

He remained silent for a moment, then suddenly looked directly at me and came right to the point, "Just why are we having this Cultural Revolution?"

From the note of urgency in his voice I could easily imagine his turbulent state of mind. And yet at that moment I myself was unclear as to the actual significance and purpose of the Cultural Revolution. I could only recite to him all the familiar statements that I had read in the papers and heard in various discussions.

The more he listened, the more puzzled he seemed to grow; his head leaned far to one side; his brows were tightly knit.

"I still don't see what this Cultural Revolution has to do with me." He waited until I had finished my stock response before he continued, carefully putting his glasses back on. "I've never been the leader in this county—not even the second in command. I've never been involved with organization, propaganda work, or any policy making. Whatever the Party told me to do, I did. I only have one head, which the Party can reform any way it wishes to. As for my family history, I've already reported it five or six times since Liberation. What's there to cover up, to lie about?"

He mumbled the last sentence to himself, and as he finished talking he bent his head, supporting it with his right hand. The scar on the back of his hand looked like a vine from which the grapes had been plucked clean; it glowed red under the light.

Neither Lao Yin nor I knew what to say. My host coughed dryly, reached into his pocket for matches, and mechanically lit his beloved pipe, which was already a shiny black from a lifetime of use.

I pulled out a pack of Front Gate cigarettes and offered it to Mayor Yin, but he shook his head and said that he didn't smoke. I lit one for myself as I tried to console him. I urged him to have faith in the policies of the Party and the people, and above all to believe in Chairman Mao's doctrine of "criticizing severely but sentencing leniently." By the time my cigarette had burned all the way down, my mouth was dry from talking. If I had continued I would have said nothing but lies.

He listened attentively, nodding his head now and then, although he could not hide a slightly bitter smile. "I'm not worried about myself," he declared frankly. "This is the only good thing about having no children. But I have feelings of regret, though I don't quite know why. It's as though I've never done anything, never contributed anything to the nation, to the people."

"You mustn't think too much," I said. "None of us must think too much. As long as each one of us does his best, we're contributing to the welfare of the country."

But he smiled sadly as he shook his head in disagreement. "When I first heard about Communism I was almost thirty years old. At that time I wasn't at all clear whether the Communist ideals would ever be realized, or what it would be like if they were. I believed only that they were better than Sun Yat-sen's doctrine of the Three Principles of the People. The Communists' style was superior to that of the Kuomintang, and Mao Tse-tung was better than Chiang Kai-shek— Chiang Kai-shek made no real effort to resist the Japanese.

"It's too bad I found out about it too late. I was inducted into the army when I was fifteen and I went through so many hardships. I was interested only in my own survival and how I could climb up and become the commander of a regiment, then a division, and eventually become a general. My only thoughts were of myself. So when someone told me that the Communists wanted to teach people to live for others and to work for the common people of China, I began to feel how insignificant and unclean I was. I felt that my life had been empty, that I had lived in vain. I remember I was once so moved that my hands began to sweat until the horse whip in my hand was dripping wet.

"But after all, I come from a lowly background and didn't have much book learning as a child, so even though after Liberation I joined several study groups, my level of culture was too low. I never could understand the doctrines of Marxism. I sometimes believe that their books were written only for the intellectuals, or that they weren't even meant for the Chinese people in the first place. Before the anti-rightist campaign the local Party organization directed me to study Liu Shao-ch'i's *How to Be a Good Communist,* and I seemed to gain something from that. After all, he speaks our language. Now we've been directed to learn the teachings of Chairman Mao. A few days ago we brought out several dusty volumes of his works from the storeroom."

I told him that Liu Shao-ch'i had been forced to step aside and that his *How to Be a Good Communist* was considered poison because he had quoted sayings from Confucius and Mencius. Mayor Yin was completely dumbfounded by this news.

"What's wrong with Confucius and Mencius?" he asked. "I once studied an article by Chairman Mao that also had quotations from Confucius and Mencius!"

"When Chairman Mao uses them that's different, of course," I said matter-of-factly. "But when other people use them it's with the ulterior motive of serving their counter-revolutionary aims."

Since I wasn't much clearer on this point than he, I hurriedly changed the subject. "Why were there discrepancies in the two reports you made about your family background?"

At this he stared at me as though he were being held forcibly by someone who would not let go.

"I did report falsely," he acknowledged frankly, his face filled with contrition. "Not long after I'd gone over to the Communists I was placed in a study group where we studied the policy of leniency toward prisoners of war. The cadre called on the people to be truthful, to empty their hearts. There was one man who took the lead in approaching the Party, and the sins he confessed were truly frightening. Execution by a firing squad would have been too light a sentence to hand down, but he was forgiven. We officers who had surrendered were moved to tears.

"Everyone fought to be the first to go to the Party cadre to talk, to confess, to empty his heart. It was as though the more evil our pasts contained, the more glorious we'd become. I was even sorry then that my father wasn't a warlord or a secret police officer! So when I filled out the forms I wrote 'landlord.' It was at least believable, since who didn't believe that all of Chiang Kai-shek's officers came from the tyrannical landlord class?

"During the land reform campaign in 1953 the working committee in my village classified my family as poor peasant, because at the time of Liberation my family had no land at all. We had some land originally, but in 1948 it had been given to my sister as her dowry. My parents lived on what I sent them, which was much more than they could earn from farming. At that time I felt that being classified as poor peasants was in fact not being truthful to the Party. My father had already died, so I wrote to the Party secretary of the county, asking that we be classified as rich peasants. Afterward, the county notified my mother that she had been changed to upper middle peasant. In fact, it was my brother-in-law who later suffered from this, since he was classified as a rich peasant because of the added farmland. So he became a member of the Black Five.* This added burden caused trouble between him and his wife, and hurt their marriage."

His voice gradually grew hoarse and finally died away, leaving behind only a tragic smile. I could find no words to comfort him and merely heaved a deep sigh.

"It's getting late." This was the first time Lao Yin opened his mouth. He had put aside his long pipe and was just sitting

---

*The Black Five (*hei wu-lei*) were landlords, rich peasants, anti-revolutionaries, bad elements, and rightists.

there with his arms folded, looking worriedly at Mayor Yin.

The wind had died down a bit, but now the pattering of the rain could be heard, sounding like spring silkworms chewing mulberry leaves. Mayor Yin stood up as though he had just awakened from a dream, put on his cap, and muttered something incoherent. Lao Yin kept shaking his head as we saw him to the door. Lao Yin offered him the umbrella by the door but he refused and strode out. We watched his tall figure disappear in the wind and rain, into the darkness of the night. Lao Yin bolted the door and turned out the light, and in silence we groped our way to bed.

The next day I left for Hanchung.

I returned to Hsingan a week later. It was sunset, and the mountain peaks, the trees, and the houses were all bathed in brilliant gold. The bus station was plastered all over with posters in large characters and brightly colored cartoons and propaganda pictures, so dazzling to the eye that one did not know where to look. With my bag in hand I strolled around the small waiting room. One look at the headlines and I knew that Mayor Yin had become the target.

I went over to the county middle school to take a look at the posters there. As I passed by the door of the theater I saw that the movie advertisements had been papered over with huge slogans. The notice "Closed in order to concentrate on revolutionary activities" was pasted over the ticket window. The area around the front door of the County Committee headquarters was deserted except for a middle-aged man, his back hunched over and his head bowed as he swept the steps, watched by a young fellow who was blowing smoke rings. Perhaps he was the secretary of the Party Com-

mittee, but I was not in the mood to ask questions. The
street seemed to be livelier than it had been a few days earlier.
There were more people walking back and forth, mostly middle school students in green uniforms with red armbands.
The color red was everywhere: red-lettered slogans, posters
in large red characters, red signboards. In the light of the
setting sun they presented a scary and menacing scene. I
discovered that the names of all the shops had been changed.
Now there was the Red Guard Department Store, Serve the
People Restaurant, Red Guard Photography Shop, Protect
the East Eatery, the East Is Red Theater, and Serve the
People Agricultural Equipment Repair Shop.

From a distance I could see a large crowd of people
standing in front of the middle school. As I drew near I
realized that a debate was going on. The crowd was so
densely packed that not even a needle could be slipped into
it. I had decided to turn back, but suddenly I heard a familiar
voice. Whose was it? To get a good look, I stood on my bag
with my back against the wall of the school. Three Red
Guards were in the midst of an argument, two against one.
The lone battler was a square-faced, bushy-browed youth
who was obviously on the defensive. His face was fiery red,
and he was cursing loudly as he mopped his brow with his
handkerchief. His opponents were elated at having gained
the upper hand; with heads held high, eyes bulging, and
spittle flying left and right, they looked like victorious fighting cocks. The more aggressive one was none other than
Hsiao Wu. His face, too, was red, and his neck was thickened
with shouting, but his manner was overbearing and his head
was held higher than anyone else's.

"I say again," the unyielding, square-faced youth was shouting, "that we should act in accordance with the policies of the Party. Since he recanted and has served the Party well, there should be no digging into past records. That is what Chairman Mao has taught us."

"Hah!" Hsiao Wu said contemptuously. "You haven't yet learned all the teachings of Chairman Mao. Chairman Mao also said that wrongs must be righted and vengeance must be exacted sooner or later. What do you say to that? Now is the time to seek revenge for our brothers!"

"You see! If he can turn against his own relative for the sake of righteousness, where do you stand?" the other one demanded fiercely.

"If one has killed then he must pay with his life. There is no other way!" Hsiao Wu pressed his point.

"A blood debt must be paid in blood!" his companion shouted.

Their sentiments were echoed by some students, and although the square-faced youth continued to argue stubbornly, he was finally shouted down.

Maybe it was due to fatigue from the long journey, but I suddenly felt dizzy and nauseated. I hastily jumped down and picked up my bag. In the dying rays of the sunset, I walked toward Lao Yin's home. All along the way cries of "The killer must pay with his life" rang in my ears.

As I reached Lao Yin's doorstep the last rays of the sun died away. I was tired and hungry. All I wanted was to lie down and rest, but as I entered the house I was upset to find two guests already sitting there. A white-haired old man about Lao Yin's age was reading from a red copy of *Sayings of Chairman Mao* in such a heavy Shensi accent that I could not make out what he was reading. The other person was an old woman, whose eyes were glued to the little red book in her hand. She remained motionless until she heard my footsteps; then she looked up, as if she had just awakened. She stared at me in surprise, her mouth hanging slack, as though her jaw were dislocated. The old man paused for a fraction of a second as he glanced at me, then continued his reading. Lao Yin stood up from the edge of the bed, nodded at me, and sat down again. He placed the little red book on his knees and stared at its cover.

I put my bag alongside the small cot where I had slept more than a week before and went to get some water to wash up. I began to regret that I had come back to Hsingan. I could have gone directly back to Peking from Hanchung, but I had come back to pick up a bag I had left behind and to buy a wooden bathtub for a friend in Peking. How could I have known I would arrive just when they were rectifying Lao Yin! He was in hot water, and having someone from outside the province staying at his home could only make matters worse. As I washed my face I made up my mind that I would leave immediately if transportation could be arranged.

Lao Yin came over to ladle out water to wash the rice, and then he busied himself with making a pot of rice porridge. When it was ready he placed it on the table along with a dish of pickled vegetables. The old man and woman stood up as if they had cast off a heavy burden, picked up the little stools on which they had been sitting, and left. As soon as they were out the door Lao Yin went to the cupboard and got out the bowl of Hunan smoked pork I had brought from Sian.

I told him that I planned to return to Peking the next day. He nodded. "It's best to leave this place as soon as possible." With that, he bent over to eat his porridge and didn't say a word about his own troubles.

We had just put down our bowls and chopsticks when a new team sent by those in charge of the study class came in. One was an elderly woman, the other a self-possessed woman about forty with short hair, very much an efficient cadre member.

"Lao Yin, have you thought it over?" the younger woman asked as she pushed open the door. Her sharp eyes swept over the dishes on the table.

"I really don't know a thing," Lao Yin replied as he cleaned up the table.

"Use your head and try to remember," she said patiently. She chose the most comfortable place to sit—beside the table, with her back to the wall—and seemed prepared to stay for a long time. The old woman sat down on the other side of the table and, taking a copy of *Sayings of Chairman Mao* from her pocket, gazed fixedly at Lao Yin.

"This only happened twenty-some years ago, so why can't you remember?" the middle-aged woman continued. "Besides, he was serving under your son. So many people knew about this, how come your son never mentioned a word to you? He was only eighteen years old, so full of life, and that evil warlord Yin Fei-lung shot him! This is class hatred; how can you not avenge that? And how did your *own* son die?

These are the accounts that the Cultural Revolution must settle."

"My son died a year before the liberation of Shensi," Lao Yin replied gently as he carefully wiped the table.

"How did he die? As cannon fodder for Yin Fei-lung! He was stubbornly anti-Communist and forced all the young boys to become cannon fodder. This is a most abominable crime! You've already reached a ripe old age, so what do you have to fear? Stand up and settle accounts with him!"

"Covering up for a relative will only add to your guilt!" The old woman also had to have her say. "Don't let his frequent visits fool you. He's like the weasel that comes to call on the chicken at New Year's time; his intentions are anything but honorable! If he has done nothing wrong, why should he try so hard to seal your mouth?"

The room was already so dark that we couldn't see each other's faces, yet Lao Yin made no move to turn on the light. He just sat silently on the edge of his bed. I was dead tired and wanted only to lie down. Finally I could hold out no longer and turned on the light. As the two women opened their books to look for a quotation, I slipped out the door and went to look for Hsiao Wu.

Apparently Hsiao Wu had established quite a reputation for himself, for I had no trouble locating him. He had become the deputy commander of the revolutionary corps, as well as director of propaganda. He occupied an office all by himself and had even been assigned a female secretary. On the door of his office was a new sign, "Propaganda Office: No Admittance Except on Business," written in red characters. All the lights were on, people were coming and going, and it appeared that they were prepared to work through the night.

Hsiao Wu was wearing a brand new uniform with a wide leather belt. His face glowed; he was the picture of a vigorous, self-satisfied young man who has made it to the top.

I was intending to ask him why he had changed his opinion of his uncle, but the female secretary kept glaring at me. I told him only that I had to rush back to Peking on important business and had to leave the town the next day. I asked if he could help me get transportation.

"Leave it to me," he declared as he patted his chest. "I'll let you know first thing in the morning."

In a period of less than two weeks Hsiao Wu had changed a great deal. The way he talked, the way he moved, reminded me of someone delivering a speech. He was filled with self-confidence—indeed, with arrogance.

Since everything was arranged, I stood up to take my leave.

"Leaving? It's still early." He ostentatiously turned up his left sleeve and looked carefully at his new watch.

I smiled, but didn't say anything, and left the Propaganda Office to take a walk alone. The street was nearly deserted even though it was only nine o'clock; most of the stores had closed and many homes were already dark. The mountain wind was blowing and the night air was as cold as ice water. A half moon hung over the mountains; the somber, cloud-covered peaks looked like crouching beasts waiting for the chance to pounce.

Heading into the wind, I walked down the road from east to west and back again. Since all the shops were locked up, there was nothing to do but go back to Lao Yin's home. The two women were still there exhorting Lao Yin, who was sitting on the edge of the bed listening politely as he smoked his long pipe. I was so tired that I couldn't stop yawning. It was almost ten o'clock. The woman who looked like a cadre member noticed me glancing at my watch, so she got to her feet, saying, "You'd better get some sleep; we'll talk again tomorrow." With that, she and the old woman quickly left.

They were, after all, mountain people, and they had genuine warmth. I was quite touched, for even though they were carrying on a reform session, they were considerate enough to let people go to bed early. In the outer provinces they often took turns interrogating from eight in the morning until late at night.

I was so exhausted that when I turned out the light and got into bed my bones ached. But before I closed my eyes I made an effort to say a few consoling words to the old man. "Lao Yin, you'd better just tell them all there is to tell. There is no night or day in their 'verbal persuasions.' They won't stop until they have achieved their goals, and why should you go through all this trouble? It's better to have faith in the Party and in the people, to clear up this matter and be done with it . . . "

My voice became lower and lower, as if I were talking to myself, and it finally died away in the darkness. After some time Lao Yin's bitter laugh broke the silence.

"But I don't know what happened, I just heard that during the war there was a soldier who disobeyed an order and Yin Fei-lung personally shot him. I didn't know the soldier and I didn't see it happen, so what can I say? If they want to get rid of Yin Fei-lung, let them go ahead and get rid of him. Why must they dig into dead issues? As for my son, he was killed fighting the Communists. What can I say?"

What could he say? This question for which there was no answer followed me into my dreams.

The next morning, to my surprise, the ingenious Hsiao Wu had actually been able to procure a letter of introduction for me so that I could get on that day's plane flight. I was suddenly transformed into a "special observer" of the revolutionary corps and didn't even have to pay for the ticket. As the plane was taking off, Hsiao Wu even came over to wave goodbye to me. I waved back through the window, but I quickly lost sight of him as the town of Hsingan disappeared into the distance. Outside the window there was only mountain after mountain, the never-ending chain of the Chinling Range.

On a windy afternoon in the spring of 1968 I was walking in Peking's Tungtan Park when I ran into a cousin of Hsiao Wu's. I had met him only once before, in Hsingan, and it was he who recognized me and called out. He was wearing a heavy cotton padded jacket and had a bag slung over his shoulder. He was sitting on a bench peeling a pear. I was pleasantly surprised and sat down beside him to chat. He had come to Peking with a group of Red Guards to file a complaint. The Red Guard Headquarters of Shensi had split into two conflicting factions, struggling with each other over the policy of "attack with reasoning and defend with force." His faction had taken the initiative of sending representa-

tives to the capital to ask for the support of the Cultural
Revolutionary Group of the Central Committee of the Communist Party.

I asked about the recent situation in Sian and about his
uncle and cousin. "Your cousin has risen even higher, hasn't
he?" I asked somewhat jokingly. "What is his position now?"

Unexpectedly, this question brought a shadow over the
young man's face.

"Things have not gone well with my cousin . . . " He
stammered slightly, as though he could not decide how much
he should tell me. "He hasn't been back home for three
months, and nobody knows where he is. My uncle is so
angry with him he has developed stomach trouble."

I felt badly for my old friend when I heard this. Hsiao
Wu's cousin said that the two of them unfortunately were
in opposing camps. Hsiao Wu's group had been fiercely involved with militant tactics, and it had been publicly announced that the group leader was to be arrested. Most likely
he had gone into hiding.

"You two made yourselves entirely too conspicuous," I
said bluntly. "Don't you see that times have changed? How
can they let you go on rebelling? Soon the Liberation Army
will take over. You young people just won't learn; you don't
realize the importance of discipline in an organization, and
you are fighting constantly for power and your own self-
interest. If you continue like this there's little chance you'll
come to any good!"

Greatly chastened by my harsh criticism of the Red
Guards, he explained defensively, "We do have our faults.
My uncle said the same things. This is my first trip outside of

Shensi. I've never asserted myself in any situation, and this time I just took the opportunity to come and see Peking. I'm not like my cousin. He's gotten in too deep and he can't pull himself out—his father said he let success go to his head. At the time of the execution of Mayor Yin he was so 'red' he was almost purple . . . "

"What did you say?" I interrupted him, not believing my ears. "They executed Mayor Yin?"

He nodded. "That was early in 1967."

"On what charges?" As soon as these words were out of my mouth I waved my hand. My heart was filled with despair and sorrow. "Never mind. I know what the charges must have been. As far-fetched as possible. When all is said and done, he was a revolutionary in the cause, so how could they have put him to death?"

"At the time everyone felt it was a necessary step for the sake of the revolution. If they didn't execute a few people they couldn't establish their authority and extend their influence. Afterward we all knew we had gone too far. There were some in our faction who wanted to settle this account for him, but the time didn't seem right, so the matter was dropped. Yin Fei-lung wasn't the only case; there were many more like him."

As we talked a sudden gust of wind swept up pieces of paper and sand and swirled them in the air. The sun had long since been driven to some unknown place, and the desolate sky was a sheet of yellow mist. I shut my eyes tight and turned my face away from the rough wind, but this boy who had grown up on the yellow sandy highlands wasn't fazed by it. When the wind was at its strongest he even excitedly threw open his arms as if he wanted to catch hold of it. When the wind had passed he picked up where he had left off.

"I arrived in Hsingan on the day of Yin Fei-lung's trial. I remember that when the verdict 'Immediate execution' was announced, Mayor Yin's head fell forward. If it hadn't been for the two Red Guards behind him, who caught hold of him, he would have fainted. His wife tried to rush up to the platform, screaming all the while, 'You people follow the policy! You must follow the policy!' But she was immediately dragged away. After that the people began to cool down. Only the Red Guards around the platform clapped and shouted. My cousin jumped right up onto the platform and started shouting slogans like 'Blood debts must be paid in blood!' 'The execution of the warlord, anti-revolutionary Yin Fei-lung is a great victory for the thought of Mao Tse-tung!' At first we shouted with him, but our voices became fewer and lower. At the time I was so choked up my chest was bursting with pain. At the final shout of 'Long live Chairman Mao!' he was joined by only one voice, and it was coming from the platform. Everyone looked up—it was Yin Fei-lung! His arms were pinned behind him, and his glasses had fallen off, but his head was high. His face was waxen, and his eyes were staring straight ahead as he shouted over and over: 'Long live Chairman Mao! Long live Chairman Mao!' We were all stunned. The only sound was his lone voice."

"Ah . . . " I drew a long breath. My chest felt as if it would burst. I was completely speechless.

"As a rule, in public trials the prisoner's mouth is gagged for fear that he might shout counterrevolutionary slogans. But someone said it wasn't necessary this time, since he probably wouldn't have the nerve to do so. And then when he began to shout 'Long live Chairman Mao!' the ones holding him didn't dare cover his mouth for fear of doing the wrong thing. Then the people at the back surged toward the platform. They completely ignored the chairman of the meeting, who was calling out, 'Intensify order and revolutionary discipline!' The Red Guards rushed up onto the platform to keep the people from going up. The chairman was afraid that a riot might break out, so he quickly ordered an immediate execution. So four or five men dragged Mayor Yin out onto a truck, and without even parading him down the street, they drove directly to the rock pile. You know the place, don't you?"

I nodded. Once when I had gone into the canyon on a cart I had passed it—sheer cliffs on both sides of a large fan-shaped area strewn with rocks and boulders, the dried-up river bed of an old mountain stream.

"They tied Mayor Yin to a wooden stake that had been stuck in among the rocks. As they pointed their rifles at him, he raised his head and shouted again, 'Long live the Communist Party! Long live Chairman Mao!' His eyes were bulging as though they would burst from their sockets, and his lips were bleeding from biting them. Everyone was scared out of their wits. How could they open fire on such slogans? They had to stop him from shouting. My cousin had a large handkerchief, so he went up and stuffed it into his mouth. Then the executioners began to fire. This time there was no shouting, no cheers. No one wanted to go up for a closer look. The body just hung limply from the wooden stake, completely alone. I turned my head. I didn't dare look. A peasant slapped me on the back and asked, 'How could they shoot him when he was shouting "Long live Chairman Mao!" like that?' "

"What was your answer?" I asked.

He shrugged his shoulders and gave a bitter smile. "I told him to mind his own business."

We both fell silent. Another burst of wind. Dusk was falling earlier than usual.

"How is Lao Yin?" I asked.

"He's dead."

Hsiao Wu's cousin said he had to attend a meeting, and he hurried off. I didn't ask how Lao Yin had died, for I was reminded of the quotation from Mao Tse-tung that was part of our daily reading: "People die all the time."

"Chairman Mao Is a Rotten Egg"

In the beginning of September 1971 my husband wrote to me from the May Seventh Cadre School* in northern Kiangsu that his period of labor reform would soon be over. He was planning to be in Nanking before the middle of the month, in time for Ching-ching's fourth birthday on the thirteenth. He would take him out to the Sun Yat-sen Mausoleum, for as he said in his letter, "It's been three years since we came to Nanking, and we've never gone to pay our respects to such historical monuments as the Ming Tombs and the Sun Yat-sen Mausoleum."

If he hadn't reminded me I would have forgotten all about Ching-ching's birthday. Since our return to China we had even forgotten our own birthdays. For me birthdays

---

*The May Seventh Cadre Schools (*wu-ch'i kan-hsiao*) were established throughout the country to carry out the principles of manual work and the study of Mao's thoughts that were embodied in the May Seventh Directive (*wu-ch'i chih-shih*), issued by Chairman Mao on May 7, 1966.

had become a thing of the past except when my colleagues reminded me at the end of each year to take my ration card and buy a catty* of Strength and Prosperity Noodles—Chairman Mao's birthday noodles.

I picked up Ching-ching at kindergarten, and on the way home I told him all about his father's plans. He was delighted to hear that he was going on an outing with his father, whom he hadn't seen for a long time. His little round face broke into a smile as he skipped along beside me.

Suddenly he looked up and asked, "Mommy, what's a birthday?"

"Your birthday is the day on which you were born," I answered, without giving it a thought. It was only when I saw the puzzled expression on his face that I realized the abstractness of the word "birthday." Since I was eight months pregnant at the time, I placed his hand on my swollen abdomen and said, "In another month the baby will be born, and the day it arrives will be its birthday."

I couldn't tell if he actually understood what I was saying, but he skipped ahead, shouting, "Birthday! Birthday!" I was hardly able to keep up with him, and by the time I reached the steps leading up to our dormitory area I was out of breath. Tiger Pass Dormitory, situated on a hill, consists of several rows of one-story buildings. The families of over two hundred faculty members of the Institute of Hydraulic Engineering live there. Our building is halfway up the hill, and climbing up and down in hot weather made me perspire profusely.

---

* A catty equals 1⅓ pounds.

Ching-ching didn't stop to talk to any of his friends, but ran straight up to our quarters. "Nai-nai!"* he shouted happily to the old woman who had come out to meet him.

My neighbor, Auntie Wang, had asked the old woman to help take care of Ching-ching and look after me during my confinement. Her surname was An, and she was from northern Kiangsu. She was a very straightforward person, and although we had only been together for a short while, the three of us were already on the best of terms.

"Nai-nai, I'm going to have a birthday. Daddy's going to take me to San San Mausoleum!"

"San San what?" An Nai-nai was over sixty and hard of hearing.

"The Sun Yat-sen Mausoleum," I managed to gasp as I caught up with them. I was beginning to regret having mentioned the outing to Ching-ching. If he were to go around telling everyone about celebrating his birthday, people would think that his parents were still full of decadent capitalist ideas. So I quickly pulled him inside the house and told him not to mention his birthday again or one day he would become an old counterrevolutionary. He couldn't understand why he mustn't talk about his birthday, but he knew exactly what an "old counterrevolutionary" was. His face tightened immediately and he nodded gravely. I felt greatly relieved and let An Nai-nai take him away to wash his hands and eat his supper.

---

*Nai-nai actually means "grandmother," but it is also a term of respect for older women.

But Ching-ching couldn't keep the good news to himself after all. After supper he went to Auntie Wang's to play and told Tung-tung, her seven-year-old son, who was just entering the first grade. Since they lived so near us, and he and Ching-ching had been together in kindergarten, they had become fast friends, playing together most of the time. Later that evening, when Auntie Wang came over to visit, the first thing she said was, "I hear that it will soon be Ching-ching's birthday. Is that true?"

"Yes," I admitted with some embarrassment.

Auntie Wang was in charge of the youngest group at the kindergarten—the three- to four-year-olds—so Ching-ching was in her group. Since she was very patient and sang well, the children were all very fond of her. Like so many Cantonese, she was lively and talkative. She had been designated as a poor citizen of the city (I never quite understood what this term stood for; people said that it meant an unemployed person, but I never had the nerve to question her about it), which made her one of the Five Red Elements* of society. Because of that she exuded self-confidence and spoke in a very loud voice. Evidently she regarded me favorably, as she often came over to visit in the evenings after finishing her household chores. Her husband and I belonged to the same teaching unit and at that time he was also working in the rice fields with the May Seventh Cadre School. Since we both had to look after a child in addition to going to work and

---

*Children of workers, poor and lower middle peasants, revolutionary cadres, Liberation Army men, and revolutionary martyrs.

doing our housework, we helped each other with shopping and other chores. And if she hadn't found An Nai-nai for me at a time when I was still new to the place, I would have been helpless.

"Tung-tung's birthday was a few days ago, on the twenty-ninth of August, but I didn't do anything to celebrate." There was an overtone of remorse in her voice. "When his daddy returns I'll ask him to take him to People's Park."

"That'll be nice," I said. "You should all go boating together in this crisp autumn weather. Just think how wonderful it would be to have a photo taken!"

"Too bad we don't have a camera."

I would have liked to lend her our Canon camera but I was afraid that she would embarrass me by refusing my offer. So although the words were on the tip of my tongue, I said nothing. About a year earlier I had impetuously offered the camera to our Party section leader, who took one look and flatly refused it. From then on I was reluctant even to take out the camera, which had been made in a "militaristic country."

Auntie Wang couldn't stop yawning. She looked very tired, so I asked, "Didn't you get any rest today after being on duty last night?"

She shook her head as she covered her mouth with her hand. There were dark circles under her eyes.

"I lay in bed all day, but I couldn't sleep!" she said as she looked around. An Nai-nai was taking a bath behind the closed kitchen door and Ching-ching was already in bed in the other room. She leaned over and whispered, "You know

Shih Lao-shih's* daughter, Hsiao Hung, don't you?"

"Of course," I said. "Isn't she in Ching-ching's class?"

Hsiao Hung's father and I were in the same department. He came from a choice background and had been a Party member for many years. Because of his role in the Cultural Revolution, he was now in charge of a study class to inspect the mid-level cadres in our provincial government. His wife was a teacher and was also performing labor in the May Seventh Cadre School. Since neither parent was in Nanking, Hsiao Hung was left in the care of the kindergarten day and night. She was a lovable little girl with pretty rosy cheeks. I had even brought her to our home to play one day during the summer.

"I'll tell you something, but you mustn't mention it to anyone!" Auntie Wang whispered in my ear.

"Of course!" I promised. I closed my door gently, then made her sit down by the desk while I sat on the edge of the bed.

"At ten o'clock last night," she continued in a whisper, leaning close to me so as not to be overheard, "after all the children were asleep, Lao Wang of the political section showed up, bringing with him Lao Shao of the broadcasting section and a tape recorder. The director of the kindergarten was with them. They told me to wake up Hsiao Hung. She was sleeping so soundly I couldn't wake her, so I had to carry her into the dining room and wipe her face with a cold wash-cloth. Even after she opened her eyes she was still only half awake. Lao Shao turned on the tape recorder. Section Chief

---

*Lao-shih means "teacher."

Wang closed the door, and then he and the director began to question Hsiao Hung. First they asked her, 'What is your father's name? What is your mother's name?' Then 'Did anyone teach you to shout reactionary slogans?' Hsiao Hung, whose eyes were still closed, kept shaking her head. After a while the director grew impatient and demanded, 'A little friend of yours said she heard you shouting a reactionary slogan . . .' " Now Auntie Wang's lips were almost touching my ear. " 'Chairman Mao is a rotten egg.' Did you shout that?" Apparently the seriousness of the situation suddenly dawned on her, because she opened her eyes—you remember her eyes, as bright and shiny as lichee nut kernels—and she stared at Section Chief Wang, then at the director, shaking her head over and over.

"They took turns urging her to confess, to tell the truth and be Chairman Mao's good little girl. They said that if she would confess that would be the end of it. Finally the director told her the name of the friend who had reported her. That seemed to jog her memory, and she burst out crying. We had to comfort her for a long time before she quieted down. I thought that would be the end of the matter, but they began to question her again, 'Why did you shout that reactionary slogan? Where did you hear the slogan? Did your daddy say it? Did your mommy say it? Did your teacher say it?' Hsiao Hung just kept shaking her head at every question. Aiya, Wen Lao-shih, you don't know how frightened I was! I was in a cold sweat!"

At this point Auntie Wang straightened up; her eyes rolled back as though she were going to faint, and she was patting her chest with one hand.

"When I stole a glance at my watch I was shocked to find that it was already midnight. The poor child couldn't take any more and couldn't keep her eyes open. When they asked her again, 'Did you hear your mommy say it?' she just closed her eyes and nodded her head. They asked her, 'When did she say it? Where did you hear it?' but she couldn't answer anymore. Finally, after much fruitless questioning, they let me carry her back to bed. The moment she was in my arms she fell fast asleep. But I haven't been able to sleep a wink. It's been on my mind all day long."

No wonder she couldn't sleep; I was dumbstruck just hearing her talk about it.

"Did you say they taped everything?"

"Of course," Auntie Wang replied. "And it will be part of her record forever."

"Her record!" I hugged myself as I felt a sudden chill in my heart. "Heavens, she's just a child!"

"Yes, not yet four; a little younger than your Ching-ching." Auntie Wang sighed.

I shook my head in disbelief. I felt, as Hsiao Hung most probably had felt, that I must be dreaming. Shih Lao-shih came from an approved background, I recalled, but his wife was from a landlord family and for that reason she tried harder in everything she did. Now their daughter had gotten into this terrible mess, and they were totally unaware of it. Poor Hsiao Hung, only four years old, and already she had all of this recorded against her. The tape would be filed away, and if in the future she did anything out of line it would be brought out to prove that she had been a "reactionary since childhood."

No wonder Auntie Wang couldn't sleep. I was so upset myself that I tossed and turned all night. Hsiao Hung's bright eyes and rosy cheeks kept appearing before me.

From then on, I asked Auntie Wang daily how things were going. First she had to make a written report, then the director of the kindergarten consulted with the school. Finally someone was sent to Hsiao Hung's mother's home in Tiench'ang County to investigate her. Now I began to worry about the mother. And poor Shih Lao-shih! All year long he traveled throughout the country investigating other people, never dreaming that his own wife would some day be the object of an investigation.

On Sunday evening, as An Nai-nai was washing the dishes in the kitchen and I was reading Ching-ching a story from the children's book *Nabbing the Secret Agent by Strategy*, Auntie Wang came over. She looked around nervously, her small eyes bright with excitement and filled with mystery. Something unfortunate must have happened to Hsiao Hung's mother. I gave Ching-ching two pieces of candy and coaxed him into An Nai-nai's room to read a book, then gently closed the door behind him.

"How are things with Hsiao Hung's mother?" I asked anxiously. I didn't even offer Auntie Wang a seat, but simply pointed to the chair at the desk. I propped up my stomach and plopped down on the bed to await the news.

"Hsiao Hung's mother?" Auntie Wang stared at me, shaking her head and waving her hands. "It's not Hsiao Hung's mother. It's Ching-ching!"

"Ching-ching?" I repeated, completely at a loss.

"Aiya, what can I say? . . . " She plumped herself down

on a chair, then, drawing it towards me, she leaned over so close that her chin almost touched my belly as she whispered, "Tung-tung told me that when he was playing with Ching-ching this afternoon he heard Ching-ching shout . . . he shouted a reactionary slogan!"

"A reactionary slogan? What slogan?" I still didn't understand.

"Aiya!" Unable to sit still any longer, she jumped up. Pressing close to my ear, she spat out the words, one by one, "He said: 'Chairman Mao is a rotten egg'!"

"What?!" I cried, springing to my feet.

"Shh! Not so loud!"

Auntie Wang caught hold of me and pressed me back onto the edge of the bed. I was completely numb, my mind a blank, as I muttered over and over, "Reactionary slogan . . . reactionary slogan . . . "

"The child's still young and can be straightened out. Speak to him. There's no need to spank him." Auntie Wang sat down beside me, trying to comfort me.

It was quite a while before I could pull myself together enough to ask, "Aside from Tung-tung, who else heard him say it?"

"I don't know," she frowned, her head tilted in thought. "I think just the two of them were playing together."

I made up my mind to talk to Tung-tung in order to get to the bottom of this. An Nai-nai was just then coming out of the kitchen, wiping her hands on her apron, as I started out of the room, dragging Auntie Wang after me. I was waddling with the weight of the child in me. "What's the matter?" An Nai-nai asked.

"We'll be right back!" I answered as we left for Auntie Wang's apartment. When Tung-tung saw the look on my face he was badly frightened. His small eyes opened wide, he waved his hands, and he shook his head vigorously. "I didn't say anything! I didn't say anything! Ching-ching said it!"

It was only after some questioning that I finally learned what had happened: That afternoon, as the two of them were playing in the garden, they had begun by calling anyone they could think of a "rotten egg." After shouting "Daddy's a rotten egg!" "Mommy's a rotten egg!" Ching-ching had let slip the name of the one person he should never ever mention.

"I'm going to give him a good spanking!" Once my fear had subsided, anger surged through me. Holding my belly I stamped angrily on the cement walk.

"Spanking alone won't solve the problem, Wen Laoshih," Auntie Wang remonstrated. "You have to start from the beginning and teach him to love Chairman Mao. You must guide him into loving our leader."

"As if I haven't . . . " I choked up at the injustice of the insinuation, and tears began to flow.

Not love Chairman Mao? How could I begin to tell her! To start with, my husband had not wanted our child to be born in a foreign country, so we had rushed back to China so he could be born here. And even before he was born his school name had already been chosen: Wei-tung—Defend Mao Tse-tung. When he was but a few months old we were lifting him up to look at Chairman Mao's portrait so that he'd recognize it as he grew up. He would laugh at the sight of his picture, and kick his legs and wave his arms. Before

he could even say "Mama" he was crying out "Mao! Mao!"
How could anyone say that he didn't love Chairman Mao?
And we, his parents, did not lag behind. In 1969, when the
entire country was fanatically promoting the Loyalty Campaign,* I went out for four hours every night after a full day's
work to take my turn at embroidering the huge portrait of
Chairman Mao. In response to the call from the rebel faction, every wall in our home, except in the kitchen and the
toilet, was plastered with Chairman Mao's portraits, poetry,
calligraphy, and the like. It was not until his wife, Chiang
Ch'ing, began to feel that all of this was too vulgar and gave
the order to stop, that we took them all down.

How could anyone say that we did not love Chairman
Mao? Why, in order to follow him we had abandoned our
families and had come to China, where we had neither
friends nor relatives. Time and again my husband told Ching-
ching that Chairman Mao was the only family we had.

"Don't cry any more, Wen Lao-shih." Auntie Wang
tried to console me. "You're so big with child now that you
mustn't get upset. As I said, Ching-ching is still young and
can be straightened out."

She talked as though Ching-ching were already a hope-
less case. All I wanted to do was cry my heart out. But I was

---

*The Loyalty Campaign (*Chung-tzu hua yün-tung*) was supposedly
initiated by the masses, but was highly endorsed by Lin Piao and his followers. Its objective was to worship and glorify Mao and promote his thought
through daily life. At the beginning and end of each work day, everyone
shouted "Long live Chairman Mao," recited his teachings, sang songs of
praise, and danced before his picture. Every school and factory had a
Loyalty Room in which were displayed many types of handicrafts, all with
one subject—Mao; and in every household the walls were to be covered with
objects related to him.

afraid that the neighbors would hear me and that the news
of the incident would spread. So I took some deep breaths
and silently wiped away the tears that kept rolling down my
face. Suddenly the baby in my womb moved, and what
should have filled me with mystery and great happiness was
only a throbbing pain. Forgetting my tears, I pressed both
hands against my belly.

"Tung-tung," Auntie Wang admonished her son, "you're
not to tell anyone about Ching-ching! If you do I'll give you
a spanking, and Ching-ching won't play with you anymore!"

Tung-tung stared at his mother with tiny eyes that re-
sembled hers. He nodded his little head repeatedly like a
grave old man.

I went home filled with anger. An Nai-nai had just finished bathing Ching-ching and was dressing him as I rushed
into the room.

"What's the matter, Wen Lao-shih?"

I began questioning Ching-ching without even answering
her. He raised his plump little face, mouth open, eyes blinking as he pulled at his wet hair; the incident was obviously
not preying on his mind.

"Tung-tung said you shouted 'Chairman Mao . . . ' " At
this point I hesitated and from force of habit looked around
before continuing in a lowered voice, " 'is a rotten egg!' Did
you say that?"

"May I hope to die!" An Nai-nai gasped as she stamped
her foot out of fright.

At this he seemed to remember. His whole face tightened
and he stared at me with fearful eyes.

"Did you or did you not say that?" I demanded again.

"Yes, I did." His voice was as soft as a mosquito's.

"Why?" I screamed angrily.

His face was now without expression. His mouth hung open foolishly and his eyes were as dull as a dead fish's. Even in my anger I felt sorry for him, but my heart was filled with foreboding. So many parents had said to me, "A child may steal or rob, but he must never ever commit a political error." Armed with this thought, I leaned over and slapped him hard on each cheek. This took him completely by surprise; he covered his face and burst into tears.

"Oh, don't be so hard on the child!" the frightened old woman said as she pulled him away from me. Ching-ching cried louder than ever, holding his tear-streaked cheeks with his hands. "Don't you ever say that again!" An Nai-nai scolded, with a set face. "Only counterrevolutionaries say such things. If you say it again I'll smack your mouth! See what you've done to your mother! Now, promise you'll never say it again."

"Won't . . . say it . . .," he managed to gasp between sobs.

"Come, let's wash your face again." An Nai-nai dragged him off to the kitchen before I could say another word.

What shall I do? I kept asking myself. Completely exhausted, I walked slowly to my room. I closed the door, leaned against the wall, and closed my eyes tightly, wishing I could shut out everything and not have to worry about a thing. The turmoil in my mind was like the rising and falling waves of a raging sea futilely searching for the land. I wasn't even sure whether I was anxious for Ching-ching or for myself. I had the sudden urge to write my husband, but I was afraid that if the letter were censored it could be used as damaging evidence. I decided it was better to wait until he came home; that would also save him a few days of anxiety. Such anxiety would, of course, pass in time, but what concerned me most was that he might be disappointed in his son. That would be a tremendous emotional blow for him. After traveling thousands of miles to come back to China, he had met with so much personal frustration. His only hope was that his son, born and raised under the red flag, would grow up as an accepted member of the eight hundred million people, living a peaceful life without the burden of any previous ideology. And now Ching-ching was but four years old, and this humble hope was already in danger of being dashed. How could my husband bear such a blow?

After much thought, I decided not to tell him about the incident—not even after he came home. But how was I to stop others from bringing it up? I was sure I could ask An Nai-nai not to say anything, and I could hint at it to Auntie Wang. Since she and my husband were from the same province, and since the Cantonese are well known for their loyalty, I was confident that she would not report the matter to the school authorities. But I wasn't so sure of her husband. He was a colleague of mine, a man with a reputation for being very progressive. Besides, he had close ties with Party members and higher officials. He had always kept me at a polite distance, even though his wife and I were close friends, most probably because I had been poisoned by an "American imperialist" education. I decided that from then on I must be extra careful not to offend him. Neither could I afford to offend Auntie Wang or, for that matter, even Tung-tung.

At the thought that I, a grown woman, had to be on

guard against a seven-year-old child, my cheeks flushed. This was all Ching-ching's doing! I was extremely angry as I walked away from the wall toward the desk. I closed my ears to the whimpering coming from the next room. The baby inside me moved again; I felt as though an electric current were running through my whole body. Hugging myself tightly, I quickly sat down.

On the desk was a huge pile of books, composed exclusively of the sayings, poems, and essays of Mao Tsetung. There were various editions: hard-covered ones, pocket books, and every other kind that was available. I sighed as I raised my head to look at the portrait of Chairman Mao hanging on the wall in front of me. He seemed to be smiling slightly, as if completely unmoved by what had just taken place. His cold, aloof look gave me a momentary fright.

At that moment the baby moved again. First I felt numb, then there was a dull pain. I held myself tightly, silently assuring my unborn child: Don't worry, when you come into the world I'll find an excuse to take that portrait off the wall.

Thus, I sat in my room, thinking, planning, and worrying deep into the night before turning out the light and going to bed.

At daybreak An Nai-nai got up to prepare breakfast. I got up at six o'clock since I had to go to the market. I had hardly slept at all, and I looked haggard; my eyes were swollen and my mouth was dry. I felt top-heavy and not too steady on my feet, and I could see that the old woman was concerned.

"You didn't sleep well," she said, "so go back to bed and I'll do the shopping."

I shook my head, muttering without even really knowing what I was saying, "His father'll be coming home soon."

"Now don't you go telling him about it!" she advised me firmly, sensing what was on my mind. "I don't think you should worry so much. What can they do to such a small child for saying something wrong, kill him? In our Huaian County the farmers always use Chairman Mao's name when they swear or take a pledge. It's worse when they start cursing! Many of them have been poor peasants for three generations, and nobody ever did anything to them!"

An Nai-nai's simple honesty comforted me, but there was no way I could make her understand the great difference in the political treatment of peasants and intellectuals.

When Ching-ching got up he was smiling just as usual, even though his eyes were slightly swollen. He'd already forgotten all about the trouble he'd caused.

"Mommy, is today my birthday?" he asked as he picked up his bowl of rice porridge.

I ignored him, my face taut. I was angry, yet amused. After all, a child is still a child. Looking at his plump little face, so innocent, I thought of his classmate Hsiao Hung, and in my mind's eye I could see a child being questioned late into the night. Only this time it was Ching-ching. The thought killed my appetite, and I couldn't taste what I was eating. An Nai-nai, trying to tempt me to eat, opened a bottle of Hangchow fermented bean curd that someone had given her. Thanks to her, I managed to force down my bowl of rice porridge, although I didn't do justice to the famous delicacy she had placed before me.

At a quarter to eight I led Ching-ching out the door, just

as the Chos, who lived next door to us, were coming out of
their apartment. Mr. Cho, meticulously dressed in his Mao
jacket, stepped briskly along with his head held high, while
thin, tiny Mrs. Cho followed behind him. The moment she
saw me she smiled.

"Good morning, Wen Lao-shih."

"Good morning!" I answered hastily, carefully scrutiniz-
ing their faces. Mr. Cho nodded at me with a faint smile,
then lifted his head again and walked steadily on. Mrs. Cho
stopped to pat Ching-ching on the head before hurrying after
her husband. I purposely slowed down, and in a little while
the Chos' two sons came out. They were already in middle
school and proudly wore Red Guard bands on their arms.
They stopped and, with smiling faces, called out "Ching-
ching" before hurrying on. These two Red Guards didn't
seem to behave any differently than usual, so I figured that
they couldn't know about Ching-ching. I was greatly relieved, but I would also have to be careful of the Cho family.

It was no accident that the school authorities had placed
us in this dormitory. There were three families in this wing:
our door was exactly opposite the Wangs', and the Chos lived
between us. Mr. Wang came from a scholarly family in Nanking, where his father had been a professor. But because his
grandfather had been an official in the Nationalist government, he had always been ultraradical in order to prove his
loyalty to the Party. People said that at the beginning of the
Red Guard movement, when the posters proclaimed that it
was forbidden to use household help, he immediately fired
Tung-tung's nai-nai. Tung-tung had weighed only two catties
and eight ounces at birth, and the old woman had taken care

of him from the time he was taken out of the incubator at the hospital. The separation was a cruel one. Four years is a long time, and they had grown very close to each other. Nainai and Tung-tung, and even Auntie Wang, broke down and cried. Mr. Wang alone, frowning silently, remained unmoved.

His was the first family in our compound to respond to the call of the Red Guards, so to show their appreciation, the Guards tore down the poster pasted on his door, to the accompaniment of drums and gongs. Later, as the number of unemployed women grew, they petitioned Premier Chou to intervene, and shortly thereafter a notice was quietly circulated that permission to hire household help could be given under certain circumstances. By then Mr. Wang had joined the May Seventh movement and was in the labor reform program in northern Kiangsu. Since Auntie Wang often had to work the night shift, she wanted to have the old woman back, but Mr. Wang was adamant. On nights when the temperature was below zero, poor Auntie Wang had to wrap Tung-tung up in so many quilts he looked like a football and carry him on her back. Sometimes when it was snowing I would take pity on the child and insist on keeping him, letting him sleep with Ching-ching. It was because of this episode that I stood in awe and fear of Mr. Wang.

Mr. and Mrs. Cho were both important Party members. Since they were always being sent out to attend meetings or to investigate questionable colleagues, they were never able to find the time to go and work on the farms. Perhaps that was the reason they were both particularly enthusiastic about the greatness of the farm labor program, loudly praising

Chairman Mao's May Seventh Directive and declaring how this path should be followed to the end. That was particularly true of Mr. Cho, who was an expert on all the political phrases and terms and spouted them fluently. Behind his back people called him the "super-leftist," but no one dared ask him to his face when he would personally follow the path of the May Seventh Directive. The Chos' sons surpassed even their parents in their zeal. At the beginning of the Cultural Revolution, when the boys were only elementary school students, they were already very proficient in organizing the other children to "search and confiscate" among the families in our dormitory. They were fierce and unrelenting, and everyone in the compound—young and old—was wary of them.

"Remember, Ching-ching," I warned him, "you're not to go and play at Auntie Cho's home anymore." But I knew that the safest way would be to try to keep him at home.

On the morning of September eleventh I woke up with great excitement; my husband would be arriving that noon. Now that what I had looked forward to for such a long time was coming true, I felt apprehensive. My rapidly beating heart grew heavy, weighing me down.

Just as I finished washing up, An Nai-nai came in with a smile to show me what she had bought. She had gotten up at four o'clock to buy fresh vegetables and fish at the Dragon Way open market. The sight of her purchases and her smiling face made me happy, but also somewhat ashamed. I had lived in China several years, but I still had not acquired the habit of giving up sleep for the sake of satisfying my appetite.

As I was about to leave for work, taking Ching-ching

along as usual, An Nai-nai said, "His daddy's coming home today, so why are you sending him to kindergarten?"

"Mommy, I don't want to go!" Ching-ching protested.

"I think you'd better go," I said after thinking it over. "Nai-nai can work better then."

He was very disappointed, but just then the Wangs' door opened and Tung-tung came out, satchel in hand, behind his mother. The moment the two children saw each other they began talking, and Ching-ching's protest was quickly forgotten. Then the members of the Cho family emerged from their door, and after a flurry of greetings, we all went our separate ways.

It was a beautiful sunny day; everything was bright and clear. The path to the kindergarten was lined with French firmiana trees, and the sunlight filtering through the leaves cast speckled shadows on the cobbled path, flitting and dancing in the breeze. Even as I stepped on the dappled shadows my mind was busily trying to analyze the facial expressions of the neighbors from whom we had just parted: The "super-leftist" had held his head high in his usual unapproachable manner. Had his wife stopped to pat Ching-ching's head? The two Cho boys had hurried away after calling out, "Auntie Wen." Had they been in a hurry to go to school or were they trying to avoid me? And Auntie Wang had called out only a brief good morning to me, then hurried off to chat with Mrs. Cho about the weather. Seeing her so friendly with this Party member, I wondered if she would tell her about Ching-ching.

As I walked and wondered my head began to ache. Ching-ching was skipping and running ahead of me. As I followed him my forehead dripped with perspiration, and my stomach tightened spasmodically. I wiped my forehead with one hand and held my belly with the other, panting heavily. When I finally reached the kindergarten, the other children were already there, and I saw Hsiao Hung sitting on the floor playing with some wooden blocks. She was wearing a pink smock on which her mother had embroidered the words "Love Labor." Suddenly she raised her head and called out, "Hi, Ching-ching's mommy." I managed to smile at her before I turned away, for my eyes were filling with tears.

When I came home at noon I was surprised to find Ching-ching sitting on his father's lap with his face wreathed in smiles.

"What's the matter with you? You look terrible!" my husband cried. He put Ching-ching down, hurried over to hold me, and made me sit down on the edge of the bed.

"Nothing," I said. "I just walked too fast."

Ching-ching stood on a chair and began to leaf through the pile of children's books on the table, exclaiming, "Look, Mommy! Daddy brought me all these books!"

I could tell at a glance that they were the usual comic books about catching special agents. I said nothing, although I really didn't like these children's books, for they fill the children's minds with the concept of spies and special agents. In Ching-ching's mind there were only two kinds of people in the world: the good ones and the spies. It was as though China had become a nation of spies.

It had been a long time since my husband and I had seen each other and there was so very much to say. But now we just looked at one another, not knowing where to begin. His hair was clipped short, his face was deeply tanned, and he looked healthy and strong. His patched blue cloth shirt and trousers had turned gray from many washings and were covered with new patches. He didn't look any different from the laborers in the commune on the outskirts of Nanking.

An Nai-nai was cooking lunch in the kitchen, and the whole house was filled with the fragrance of fish cooked in wine. My husband smiled faintly and looked at my large belly, but all he said was, "The food smells good!"

"Lunch is ready!" An Nai-nai called. "Go wash your hands, Ching-ching."

Ching-ching reluctantly left his books, climbed off his chair, and went into the kitchen.

"You must be careful when you buy children's books," I quickly told my husband. "Don't buy any that have too many pictures of Chairman Mao."

"Don't worry," he answered with an understanding smile. "My colleagues have already warned me that it's best not to buy comic books like those about the heroes Lei Feng and Wang Chieh, as there are pictures of Chairman Mao on almost every other page. Children have caused a lot of trouble by spoiling the Chairman's picture when they color the books."

He leaned closer to me, lowering his voice to a whisper, "My colleagues remove the pages with Chairman Mao's pictures on them before they give the books to their children. I've done the same thing. Just don't say anything about it. We've got to be very careful with Ching-ching. He's at a difficult age, understanding the words we say, but not fully comprehending their meaning. Don't let him draw on the ground, and don't give him any chalk or pencils. If he should get into trouble, with our background we couldn't clear ourselves even if we jumped into the sea to try to wash our sins away. And now with the old woman living with us in the house, we must be extra careful. These days one must always be on guard."

"Yes, yes," I hastily agreed, avoiding his eyes as I felt another dull pain.

During lunch both my husband and An Nai-nai kept heaping fish and vegetables into Ching-ching's bowl.

"Ching, have you been a good boy at home?" his father asked him. "Have you done anything naughty?"

"No!" Ching-ching declared unhesitatingly, busily stuffing fish into his mouth.

An Nai-nai looked at him, then went on eating without saying a word.

My husband kept urging me to eat more fish. "A pregnant woman must eat fish. It contains a lot of calcium and phosphorous."

I felt a bit guilty when I looked at his bright, cheerful face, filled with the joy of being home again. As I listened to him tell how he had learned to cut hair and patch clothes I pulled myself together and finished my lunch.

On my way back to work in the afternoon I met Tung-tung's father. He was pushing his bicycle along with one hand and balancing a large covered food tray with the other. One look and I knew that he had bought roast duck from the famous restaurant Ta San Yüan. He nodded politely as I greeted him, his white teeth showing up against his dark face.

After dinner that evening, while my husband was waiting

for his bath water to heat, Ching-ching and I took our stools out into the garden as usual to sit for a while. In Nanking, as soon as September arrives the mornings and evenings grow cool, and it is very pleasant to sit outside after dinner. During the summer many of the families even move out into the garden to eat their dinners. Every day at twilight our compound was crowded with tables and chairs, as the teachers and their entire families sat around in T-shirts and shorts, a fan in one hand and a pair of chopsticks in the other. The evenings would ring with their laughter and spirited conversation.

That night we were sitting in our usual spot under the Wangs' kitchen window. Auntie Wang, who always came home from work late, was just then beginning to cook dinner. The smell of vegetables and oyster sauce wafted out through the window. As she walked around the kitchen she was humming a tune that was unfamiliar to me—this was unprecedented; I had always thought that she knew only revolutionary songs. I could see just the upper half of her body; she was wearing a bright red short-sleeved blouse, her hair was newly trimmed, and she was smiling as she worked. She was a typical southern woman, always dressed in up-to-date clothes, but this was the first time I'd seen her in such bright colors. Seeing her so happily occupied, I hadn't the heart to greet her. Many of the teachers who had just returned from work were outside in the compound busily greeting one another. It seemed noisier than a special holiday.

About nine-thirty, when Ching-ching and An Nai-nai were already in bed and my husband and I were just preparing to retire, there suddenly came the sound of a child crying. I recognized Tung-tung's voice and, startled, began to put on the blouse I had just taken off.

"Don't meddle in other people's affairs," my husband said.

"I'll just take a look," I answered as I hurried to open our door. I saw that Mrs. Cho had already poked her head out her door to listen.

"What's going on?" I asked her. "Why is Tung-tung crying so hard?"

"I don't know," she answered, as she opened her door a little wider.

Tung-tung's father had been talking in a loud voice, and suddenly, as though someone had pulled the plug on the radio, there was no more sound. Even Tung-tung's crying trailed off and become a soft sobbing. Mrs. Cho and I listened for a while but we could hear nothing more, so we closed our doors.

"What was it?" my husband asked as I came back to bed.

"Nothing," I answered. "Tung-tung was crying."

And yet I was worried. We had been neighbors for several years and I had seldom heard Tung-tung cry. The Wangs loved their son dearly and never raised their voices when talking to him. I worried that it might have something to do with Ching-ching, and I didn't sleep well that night. I woke constantly, the child within me so heavy that I had a hard time breathing.

The next day was Sunday. I purposely left our door open, hoping that Tung-tung would come over to play, but I neither saw nor heard anyone from the Wang family. I urged my husband to take Ching-ching to the Ming Tombs and the Sun Yat-sen Mausoleum, but he said that since it was Sunday it would be too crowded; he would take the boy on the following day, which was his birthday. Meanwhile, it had been a long time since he had gone downtown, so right after an early lunch he took Ching-ching and went off light-heartedly.

In the afternoon the coal man delivered our ration of a hundred coal bricks, which he piled up right in front of the door. An Nai-nai would not let me help as she carried them, four at a time, into the kitchen and stacked them under the sink. Since I couldn't help her, I began to sweep up the coal dust. The Wangs' door was slightly ajar, and Tung-tung peeped out at me.

"Tung-tung, where's your mother?" I asked as I swept.

"Taking a nap," he whispered, opening the door a little wider to stick out his head.

"Why were you crying last night?" I asked in a whisper.

He gazed at me silently, his eyes blinking.

"Your father didn't scold you, did he?"

He hesitated, then said slowly, "He spanked me." He blinked, as though he were still feeling the hurt.

"Really!" I cried out in surprise, dropping the broom and knocking over a coal brick, which shattered into pieces.

"See what you've done!" An Nai-nai came rushing over, very upset at the waste. She snatched the broom away from me and did the sweeping herself.

"Why did your father spank you?" I walked over to him. Pressing close to the door, I whispered, "Did you do something bad?"

"I said a reactionary slogan," he admitted ingenuously.

"What?" I gasped. "It was *you* who said it? Now exactly who did say it, you or Ching-ching?"

He nodded, then shook his head.

"I won't say it again. Daddy told me not to tell anyone . . . "

"Tung-tung!" Mr. Wang suddenly called out from inside, frightening the boy. Tung-tung pulled his head back in and slammed the door.

"What's happened?" An Nai-nai had heard only part of the conversation. She straightened up, forgetting her sweeping, and stared at me inquisitively. "Who said it?"

"Maybe it wasn't Ching-ching after all." I began to feel a glimmer of hope. Just then, since the door had been slammed hard against my belly, I felt a stab of pain.

"What's the matter?" the old woman asked as she saw me clutch my belly with both hands.

"It's nothing," I answered reassuringly. Then I felt my womb constricting into a tight ball and I was frightened. "I'll go and lie down for a while."

But how could I rest? I paced up and down in my room, holding my belly as I anxiously waited for my husband and son to return. I couldn't be sure how much time had passed before I heard Ching-ching's voice calling out, "Mommy!" When An Nai-nai hurried out to open the door, he came rushing in, a box in his hand. "Mommy, new shoes! Daddy's going to take me to the Mausoleum tomorrow on my birthday!"

I rushed over and grabbed him. "Come with me," I cried, dragging him into the bedroom. My husband immediately followed us inside, asking over and over, "What's the matter?"

I pulled Ching-ching over to the desk and with a severe look pointed to Chairman Mao's portrait, demanding in a low voice, "Ching-ching, I want you to tell me the truth. Tung-tung said that he was the one who said the reactionary slogan. Now did he or didn't he?"

The moment he heard the words "reactionary slogan" and looked at Chairman Mao's portrait his face froze.

"Reactionary slogan? What reactionary slogan?" My husband grew tense and agitated as he grasped Ching-ching's shoulders tightly.

"I didn't say it!" Ching-ching shook his head repeatedly as he gazed fearfully at his father. "I didn't say it. It was Tung-tung . . . "

"Ah!" I let out a sigh of relief. I felt as though a weight had been lifted, and my heart soared.

"What did he say? Tell me quickly!" His father frantically shook him by the shoulders. "What did he say? Where did he say it?"

"In the yard," Ching-ching stammered, pointing to the window. "Tung-tung dared me . . . to say Chairman Mao . . . a rotten egg. But I wouldn't say it. It was Tung-tung who said it!"

"When was this? Answer me right now!" I demanded impatiently.

"I think it must have been yesterday afternoon," An Nai-nai interrupted. She had followed us unnoticed into the room. "They were playing in the yard for a while."

"Yesterday?" Stunned and disappointed, I felt as if I had fallen from a cloud.

"What? Children saying reactionary words like that!" My husband's face was dark with anger as he shook the child fiercely. Ching-ching was so frightened he burst into tears.

"Stop crying!" my husband shouted. "How about it? Did you say it or didn't you? Answer me right this minute!"

Ching-ching cried even louder. I began to feel faint. An Nai-nai caught hold of me, crying out, "Oh, oh, look at her face!" I was taken to the hospital that very day and after a whole night's ordeal I gave birth, a couple of weeks early, to our second child.

My colleagues often remark with envy, "Wen Lao-shih, your two sons have the same birthday." I invariably answer with a smile, "Thanks to Chairman Mao."

And truly I did have Chairman Mao to thank, for from then on Auntie Wang became my very close friend, and even her husband nodded and smiled whenever he saw me.

Night Duty

Liu Hsiang-tung strode into the dining hall of the collective farm, a large bowl tucked under his arm and a pair of chopsticks in his hand. The place was already packed, with long lines in front of each food-stall window, even the one in the far corner where soup was usually sold. There was good reason why the hall was more crowded than usual that night: the teachers who had just arrived that afternoon had come in for dinner after being assigned their beds, and those who were returning to Nanking the next morning lined up early to enjoy their last meal at the farm. Since there was no more room at the tables, most of the people were eating their food standing up. Hsiang-tung took his place at the end of one of the lines and dug into his pocket for his rice and vegetable coupons as he studied the menu pasted on the wall.

The day's menu, written with black ink on a piece of bright red paper, had caught his eye at once. To express their

welcome to the newcomers and their farewell to those who
were leaving, the kitchen staff had prepared several special
dishes: a meatball called lion's head, sweet-and-sour pork,
and the saltwater duck of which Nanking people are so
proud. The menu stimulated his appetite, and as he watched
the people around him devouring their food, his stomach
began to growl. His appetite had greatly increased since his
return to China the year before. He was eating twice as
much and having no more stomach trouble; in America he
had always been concerned that he might have ulcers. The
thought struck him that a man's stomach really adapts in
quick order.

> Soldiers of the revolution, each must remember
> To observe the three regulations and eight points:
> First, obedience in every action . . .

The farm's broadcasting had begun. Hsiang-tung did not
need a watch to know that it was five-thirty. Every morning
the loudspeakers blared out "The East Is Red" to rouse
everyone out of bed; then there were revolutionary songs for
relaxation during lunchtime and work breaks; and finally
"The East Is Red" sent everyone off to bed again. Life was
thus regulated, never changing, making a watch entirely
superfluous. During his first days in Nanking, before he became accustomed to the shrill loudspeakers, Hsiang-tung felt
that they violated his personal freedom, interfered with his
train of thought, and virtually forced him into conforming.
He had even toyed with the idea of mentioning these objec-
tions to the comrade leader as a suggestion for improvement.

But he soon discovered that the broadcasting was an integral part of daily life in New China, so he forced himself to accept it, eventually learning to take it in stride. Once, during rice planting season, when the work was heavy and especially tiring, he had actually fallen asleep before the broadcast ended.

"Hurry! Hurry! We're all out of saltwater duck! Cabbage is three cents a plate."

This shout greeted him as he reached the window. Peering in through the small opening, Hsiang-tung could see that all the good food had indeed been given out, so he had to be satisfied with two small dishes of sliced meat with greens and some rice. Holding his bowl carefully, he looked around for a place by a window, where it would not be so crowded, to stand and eat.

"Liu Hsiang-tung! Come join us!" Lao Ho, from Hsiang-tung's dormitory, was signaling with his chopsticks. Lao Ho and three or four colleagues from Hsiang-tung's department had a table to themselves and were already eating heartily. They squeezed over to let him have a corner of one of the benches.

"You're late. The duck is already sold out," said Lao Ho.

"It doesn't matter," Hsiang-tung said with an indifferent shrug. Being a "grasslander"* he still could not appreciate saltwater duck and found the plain cooked duck of his native Taiwan much tastier. From the piles of bones at both ends of the table, he could see that the others had all eaten duck.

"Hsiao Liu, will you be getting into the classroom when

---

*A Taiwanese peasant.

you return?" a comrade sitting opposite him asked, as he
spit out a piece of bone and noisily scraped his bowl clean.

"Assisting in first-year college math," Lao Ho answered
for him, enviously.

Hsiang-tung muttered an acknowledgment and made no
further comment as he pretended to be engrossed in his food.
The policy of rotating labor not only disrupted teaching
schedules but also caused many teachers to lose their jobs
upon their return from a period of labor. Naturally the
teachers were envious of anyone who had classes to go back
to. Hsiang-tung himself was eager to get back to the classroom, but since the universities had just started taking in
students again, there were only first-year classes, so he would
have to wait until the third year before it was decided
whether he would be able to teach his specialty. Rather than
remain idle for two years, he had urgently requested that he
be placed on the frontlines of teaching. His group leader
responded by putting him down for a so-called assistantship,
which was to begin as soon as Hsiang-tung returned from
his period of labor. In reality the job was to assist the math
teacher by helping the students with their lessons during
classes and in the dormitories.

Hsiang-tung's earnest determination to dedicate his en-
ergies to the socialist fatherland enabled him to ignore being
laughed at for using his talents at such a low level. He had
even brought along a number of reference books so he could
prepare himself while he was still at the farm. As luck would
have it, there was a young teacher in the same labor group
who had just come from assisting in a math course. Hsiang-
tung had immediately asked his help and advice. At first the

young man was aghast at the large pile of books; then he burst out laughing. At the first opportunity he took Hsiang-tung aside and informed him that first-year mathematics began with decimal points and addition, and that even when the students graduated, they would not be up to taking calculus, let alone more sophisticated subjects.

"If you can make them understand that zero point one added to zero point one equals zero point two, and that one-half added to one-half does not equal one-fourth, you'll have done your job."

This revelation greatly disappointed Hsiang-tung. He carefully tied up his books, placed them under his straw mattress, and never again mentioned his assistantship. He knew that he could not blame his disappointment on the students—they were assigned to the university to study mathematics, and it was no fault of theirs. What was it then? Why was he so upset and disheartened? He wasn't able to find the answer, and his distress became a lead weight on his heart.

"Comrades, attention!" The revolutionary songs were suddenly broken off for a report. "Tonight at seven o'clock sharp all comrades will please come to the dining hall for a meeting to evaluate the achievements of these three months of labor. We shall also want to welcome the new group of teachers who have joined us in following Chairman Mao's May Seventh Directive. After the commune Party Committee makes its report, each study group representative will report what his group has learned from this period of labor. There will be group discussions after the general meeting ends. Please be on time."

Everyone had known about this meeting for some time,

so the announcement aroused no excitement.

"It's the last night, so let us hope the meeting won't last too late." So saying, Lao Ho picked up his bowl and was the first to leave.

"What I've learned is exactly the same as last time, so I'll finish what I have to say in two minutes," a colleague sitting next to Hsiang-tung said lightly. He had finished eating, his white porcelain bowl already scraped clean. Suddenly he turned to Hsiang-tung, "This is the first time you've followed the May Seventh Directive. You must have acquired many deep impressions, so you can give a long speech tonight."

At the word "speech" Hsiang-tung reddened slightly, and said hurriedly, "I'll wait until I get back to Nanking to talk. Since I'm on duty tonight, the group leader has given me permission to miss the meeting."

"You really should attend," another colleague said considerately, "since you'll be going back to Nanking tomorrow. If you go on duty tonight you won't be able to catch up on your sleep. It's not worth it."

"It doesn't matter; the loss of a night's sleep won't bother me."

In fact, it was just such self-serving motivation on everyone else's part that had given Hsiang-tung the opportunity to take the watch that night. Having attended the same kind of meeting three months before, he had deliberately sought a way to absent himself from this one. At the earlier meeting he had listened to the previous group of teachers get up and expound emotionally on the effects of their having joined in the reeducation process under the poor, lower, and middle peasants in northern Kiangsu province. They had waxed enthusiastic about how their views of life had changed and how their convictions had completely turned around. For them it had been a rebirth. Some teachers had even wept profusely, and he himself had been so moved by what he heard that he clenched his hands into tight fists and his palms were wet with perspiration.

The blink of an eye, and three months had passed. Now he dreaded the thought of this meeting, for he knew that when the time came he could not be like the others—emotional, eloquent, singing praises, just like players in a splendid drama.

But his colleagues intended no sarcasm. Hsiang-tung was aware of his own speech-making talent. A few years earlier in the United States, during the Tiao-yü T'ai movement,* he and several like-minded friends had talked all the way from Berkeley to Chicago. From platforms, car tops, or any place where he could stand, he had spoken for hours on end. What supported him then was not only heartfelt patriotism but also a beautiful ideal, for which he stayed up nights to study the works of Lenin and Mao Tse-tung, always taking copious notes. Fearful of being investigated by the FBI, he did not dare to close his eyes at night unless his papers were safely under his pillow.

He reflected upon those enormously exciting days. By comparison, life after his return to his own country had indeed been quiet and uneventful. Except for these three

---

*A group of eight small islands on the oil-rich continental shelf near Taiwan. In 1971 overseas Chinese launched a campaign to protect China's sovereignty over the islands after Japan proclaimed ownership.

months of personal involvement in farm labor, the rest of his time had been entirely devoted to the Anti-Lin Piao campaign and study sessions. He had spent six whole months studying a thin volume, *The State and Revolution*, poring over each word and sentence, almost memorizing the entire book. Initially he had joined the discussions, especially after discovering that a great many teachers hadn't the slightest idea of the inevitability of "the withering away of the state mechanism" and the future of Communism. He had quoted all sorts of theories and sayings to prove not only the possibility but the inevitability of this future society. The more he talked, the more drunk he became with the ideal of a utopian world. Once he even lost track of how long he had been talking, only to discover that one of his colleagues was fast asleep. The discussion leader, yawning, had forced a smile when his eyes met Hsiang-tung's. Maybe this was what had earned him the reputation of "speech-maker."

What pained him, however, was not his nickname, but the truth about these higher-level intellectuals. Little by little, it dawned on him that they were given to discussing for the sake of discussion alone; that what they said was not what was actually in their hearts; and, furthermore, that they often used questions in order to pour out their own frustrations. This last realization hurt him the most, and he could not help but begin to doubt: Here in the acknowledged center of the world's revolution, just how many people truly believed in the theories of Marx and Lenin and the thought of Mao Tse-tung? Like so many other questions, this one had no answer. So as his reputation as a "speech-maker" spread, he actually grew more reticent.

"Take your time. Eat slowly."

One by one his colleagues left the table, and soon Hsiang-tung found himself alone. Just a few people were scattered around the dining hall, and the stillness was broken only by the revolutionary songs blaring from the loudspeaker. Someone sat down on the bench opposite him. It was the young peasant hired by the farm to weave baskets. With a grin at Hsiang-tung, the young man used his aluminum lunch box to push away the bones on the table and clear a space for himself. All he had were three large *mantous,** which he took out of his lunch box, and a dish of greens. Hsiang-tung glanced again at the bones strewn all over the table and was too embarrassed to look back at the man opposite him, who was by then devouring one of his *mantous.*

"Are you going back to Nanking tomorrow?" the young man asked.

"Yes. How about you? Will you be going home to Huaian soon?"

The peasant stuffed in two large mouthfuls of greens with his chopsticks before answering. "Not certain yet. After I finish the baskets on your farm, if there's no more work around here, then I guess I'll go back." With that, he picked up the second *mantou.* His cheeks were all puffed out, one higher than the other. His large, round face was deeply tanned, and he stared out from under heavy black eyebrows at the *mantou* in front of his nose.

Hsiang-tung had passed the time of day with the man before and knew that he was called Wei-tung—Defend Mao

---

*Steamed buns, which are the staple food of north China.

Tse-tung—a popular name adopted after the Cultural Revolution, as was Hsiang-tung—Toward Mao Tse-tung—for that matter. Hsiang-tung also knew that the man was from a poor peasant family. He looked to be in his early twenties, and since he hardly ever talked or paid any attention to others, he was not well liked. The farm treasurer often complained behind his back that he was a very lazy worker. It all stemmed from the fact that the contract between the farm and his commune was based on an hourly wage, not on piecework. And so he would often take his own sweet time, spending two or three days to complete one basket. Once the treasurer—who was an old Party member—simply couldn't take it any longer and tried to negotiate a new contract, based on piecework. He met with a flat refusal: "Contract labor? That's Liu Shao-ch'i's revisionist line. Wasn't the Cultural Revolution supposed to do away with that line of thought? Chairman Mao tells us always to trust in the people, to rely on the poor and lower-middle peasants." Everything the peasant said was strictly in accordance with Mao's teachings, and the treasurer, his face and ears a bright red, could find nothing more to say. Although Hsiang-tung had learned this secondhand, it made him regard the man differently.

"You've been away for quite some time. Aren't you homesick?" Hsiang-tung asked as he scraped away at his rice bowl.

The man grunted and raised his heavy eyebrows. It was not until he had swallowed the food in his mouth that he answered, coldly, "Going back will only mean more labor—land labor."

Hsiang-tung nodded. He scraped the remaining kernels of rice into his mouth and stood up to go. As he was about to lift his right leg over the bench he heard a dry laugh.

"Your kind of labor, huh!"

Hsiang-tung was so stunned by this comment that his face turned red. But the man seemed to be talking to himself, muttering very softly as he stared at the last remaining *man-tou*, a corner of his mouth lifted in a sneer. Picking up his bowl, Hsiang-tung pushed aside the bench and walked away in silence.

May nights in northern Kiangsu are cool and mild. A half moon hung on the edge of a sky with just a sprinkling of stars, and the sparsely scattered lights of the farmhouses made the sky seem especially vast and lofty. The plains spread out endlessly, far and wide. Hsiang-tung was strolling alone, holding his arms behind his back. The water in the ditches on either side of the road trickled into the rice fields, and in the boundless quiet the sound was discordant yet familiar. Everything about this night served to arouse in him memories of his homeland. At night in his old hometown of Hualien it would be the time for the insects to buzz and the ocean breezes to blow. There the mountains would be shadowy and obscure, and the moon would seem low enough to touch with one's hand. There was no similarity to these vast and all-encompassing flat plains, which made him feel infinitely small, to the point of helplessness. In truth, he could not say when this feeling of helplessness had set in, but it was certainly intensifying as the days passed. He could not help being surprised that within a year of his return to the fatherland his state of mind should have undergone such a great change. He seemed to be getting old before his time. How long was it since he and some close friends, all determined idealists, had stood facing the icy cliffs of the Grand Tetons and recited Chairman Mao's poem "Snow"? Loudly and clearly they had sung the words, "For men of talent the time is now."

Where had this proud, brave spirit disappeared to? Back then he had given up his doctoral thesis and would gladly have forfeited his life in defense of the sacred territory of Tiao-yü T'ai. But what had happened to Tiao-yü T'ai since then? He had once posed this question to a colleague at the university. The man had scratched his head for a moment before replying. "Tiao-yü T'ai? Isn't that located south of Peking? I think that's the place where they entertain the higher-echelon officials and visiting dignitaries." Hsiang-tung never mentioned it again.

At times he wondered if he were guilty of being an immature leftist who lacked dispassion, one whose strong patriotic emotions had deteriorated into regret and disillusionment. When he returned in 1973 he had been filled with an intense fighting spirit. But during his first two weeks in Peking, in the midst of his sightseeing, he discovered that nothing at all was known about the situation in Taiwan. Whenever Taiwan was mentioned, the middle-echelon cadremen would only quote outdated information and statistics. Then they would say that the Taiwanese eked out their living by selling their children or they would predict that as soon as the fatherland decided to "liberate" Taiwan, all the people would rise and welcome the conquerors with food and drink.

Hsiang-tung was so shocked that he stayed up all night writing a long memorandum, which he sent to the State

Council the day before he left Peking. He also called on the Taiwan Democratic Self-Government League, only to discover that their knowledge and way of thinking were separated from his by at least a generation. They were not only ignorant of the average per-capita income of an ordinary Taiwanese laborer but also unaware of the actual significance of "self-government." He was so upset and angry that he stalked out without even sipping a mouthful of tea. Thinking back now, he sorely regretted his actions.

His memorandum was like a stone cast into the ocean. Still, in the editorial for the National Day of 1973, the Taiwan compatriots were referred to as "blood brothers," and there was a greater feeling of warmth and intimacy. Although this was only a verbal embellishment, it comforted Hsiangtung considerably. Not long afterward he heard people say that this expression had been added because Premier Chou had received a suggestion from a Taiwanese who had returned on his invitation. It was also said that this Taiwanese had even been an ardent supporter of the Taiwan Independence Movement, which was considered an anti-revolutionary group by the state. Nobody knew whether this rumor was true or not, but it made one think. Hsiang-tung often asked himself what, after all, was the best possible way for overseas students to make a contribution to their homeland.

Hsiang-tung sighed deeply. A lone star seemed to be staring mutely down at him. The night wind was rising, and growing colder with each gust. The farm dormitory stood in silence, most of its lights extinguished. Hsiang-tung's watch read almost half past ten, time for him to go on duty. He hurried to the duty office, which was to the east of the dormitory area, alongside the agricultural equipment store-room. Yellow light was streaming through the closed windows. Hsiang-tung pushed open the door and went in. Lao Fu was sitting under the light, carefully cutting open an empty tin can. On the table beside him were an unfinished kerosene stove, an awl, a round mallet, and several other tools.

"Hey, Hsiao Liu," Lao Fu muttered as he peered over his glasses, his hands still manipulating a pair of shears.

Hsiang-tung returned his greeting and sat down across the table from him. They had shared night duty once before; on that occasion, too, Lao Fu kept himself busy making kerosene stoves. The stoves had earned Lao Fu quite a reputation in the school and had made him a very popular man. It was said that he had made more than a dozen during the latter part of the Cultural Revolution and had given them all to the people who needed them most.

"Since you've successfully completed your stint under the May Seventh Directive and you'll be leaving tomorrow for Nanking, I'll treat you to my home-cooked noodles with eggs." Lao Fu spread out the open tin can on the table and began flattening it with the mallet.

"You treated me last time, so tonight it should be my turn," said Hsiang-tung, opening one of the desk drawers to look at the noodles and eggs that had been placed there earlier. There was also a copy of Lenin's works.

"All right," Lao Fu agreed, "but since I have all the other ingredients, I'll do the cooking."

He was, after all, still the one who thought of everything. Hsiang-tung was embarrassed, for he had forgotten all about the condiments and other necessary ingredients. He took out the book and closed the drawer. Lao Fu began to punch holes in the piece of tin, pounding intently. Hsiang-tung's eyes followed every movement of the awl; with each punch another hole appeared, always the same size, very quick and neat.

Upon his arrival at the farm Hsiang-tung had heard the story behind this craft of Lao Fu's. Lao Fu had been a talented student at Central University, and he subsequently joined the teaching staff there not long after Liberation. He quickly rose to the position of senior lecturer, and on the eve of the Cultural Revolution he was a nominee for the position of associate professor. Unfortunately, toward the latter part of the Cultural Revolution, at the very beginning of the Cleansing of the Class Ranks,* someone sent in his name as a suspected member of the Three Principles of the People Youth Corps† while still a student at Central University. He was also accused of lying about his age. The leadership, following its policy of "better to believe that there is than there is not," formed a special committee to begin an investigation.

Two years passed without unearthing any evidence against him. The four or five members of the special committee took turns going to his hometown to investigate, and they also went to other provinces to interview some of his old classmates; but they did not turn up a single thing. But even without any actual proof that he had participated in the

*Cleansing of the Class Ranks (*ch'ing-li chieh-chi tui-wu*), the purging of those who did not follow Chairman Mao's revolutionary line.

†A Nationalist organization based on Sun Yat-sen's Three Principles of the People.

Youth Corps, they dared not let him go, so he was kept "dangling" indefinitely. Naturally, as the accused, he was the only one who suffered. During the "Cleansing" period he was jailed for six months and was then sent to a term of supervised labor. Finally, along with all the other teachers of the university, he was dispatched to northern Kiangsu to establish the May Seventh School collective farm.

Since then the One Attack and Three Antis,* Anti-Lin Piao, and other campaigns had been launched one after the other, and the school had had no time to pay any attention to Lao Fu. The whole affair was left unfinished, and the political hierarchy seemed to have forgotten that he ever existed. Meanwhile, he remained optimistic, always good-natured and even-tempered, and never despaired. His wife, however, tried to kill herself. She had been investigated three or four times and had not heard a single word from her husband (nor, for that matter, had she been told what crime he may have committed). In desperation she threw herself into the river, but luckily she was rescued. When Lao Fu received word from his relatives, he did not betray the slightest emotion. If the officials in his hometown had not notified the authorities at the school that his guilt-ridden wife was under suspicion for having attempted suicide, no one in the school would have known about it.

While he was in isolation and under investigation Lao Fu became interested in making kerosene stoves. He first remade the one he had been given to use. Then during his labor

---

*One Attack and Three Antis (*i-ta san-fan*), a campaign launched in 1970. The One Attack was against the counterrevolutionaries; the Three Antis were against corruption, waste, and opportunism.

reform period he searched out old empty tin cans wherever he could find them, and cut and pounded them whenever he had a little spare time. While his hands were thus occupied, he was oblivious to everything going on around him.

"Say, Lao Fu, I heard some of your colleagues talking; it seems that the school is considering setting you up with some classes this fall." Ever since hearing Lao Fu's story, Hsiang-tung had been very sympathetic toward the older man. He had looked forward to reporting this bit of news.

He never dreamed that Lao Fu's only response would be a disinterested "Is that so?" Lao Fu's eyes never left his hands, as he continued to poke holes. Hsiang-tung gazed at his hunched back and his bent head, the prematurely white strands of hair catching the light. He could restrain himself no longer.

"You've been a teacher for so many years," he said compassionately. "Don't you feel you're wasting your talents, spending all your time working on the farm and making kerosene stoves instead of being in class?"

"I rather like living on the farm," Lao Fu answered, this time putting down his work. He raised his head and looked at Hsiang-tung through his glasses, a half smile on his face. "And as for waste, you talk as though there are only a few things being wasted!"

How true! thought Hsiang-tung.

"I think the farms should be shut down," Hsiang-tung spoke out frankly. "In the future, when there are more students, how will they be able to spare the teachers? Besides, it's a financial loss! None of the other socialist countries— even our beloved Albania—ever did this. Having every university set up a collective farm is a waste of manpower and resources."

"The Chinese Communists have always done what others before them have never done," Lao Fu stated solemnly. Then he smiled. "And as for losing money, that isn't even worth mentioning. During the past three years we have lost more than thirty thousand a year, and that's only the investment in seeds, fertilizer, and agricultural equipment; it doesn't include the teachers' pay. Just think: we have an average of one hundred people on the farm, and a year's produce can only feed these people for six months. So how can we avoid losing money? And that doesn't take into account what's been stolen."

Hsiang-tung frowned, as he recalled that on his arrival at the farm the committee chairman had held a meeting to decide on the night duty schedule. The need for a night watch had come as a great shock to Hsiang-tung: Chairman Mao had ordered the teachers to come and learn from the poor and lower-middle class peasants, and since they were to be surrounded by these people, what was the purpose of the patrols? But there had been a duty watch every night, and the strongest men had been chosen for this assignment. As a result there was never enough labor in the fields to finish the work. Yet, even with these precautions, thefts often occurred, until even Hsiang-tung felt let down. At this point in his thoughts, he seemed to hear the dry laugh of the young peasant at dinner.

"Intellectuals need to participate regularly in labor," Hsiang-tung stated emphatically, "but the universities really needn't carry the load of a large farm."

"Chairman Mao had said, 'The May Seventh Directive should go on forever,' " Lao Fu quoted in even tones. Then he picked up his awl and started punching holes again. "His many years of revolutionary experience have taught that only labor can change one's thoughts."

Labor, labor—Hsiang-tung mulled the word over, suddenly feeling that it was meaningless. Aside from posing for photographs, he thought, it must be years since Chairman Mao has touched a rake, yet he alone has kept his youthful revolutionary spirit and is still going strong at his age. He must have a secret, thought Hsiang-tung, and it pained him that Mao was unwilling to share it with the people. A pity! Sighing deeply, Hsiang-tung stood up, and, with his arms behind his back, he began to pace around the duty room. Tap! Tap! The sound of Lao Fu's awl hitting the tin plate was dry and monotonous. Hsiang-tung tried his best not to look at him or to listen to that empty sound. He looked up and began counting the beams: one, two, three . . . , one, two, three . . .

"Shall we go and make a round?" Lao Fu had stopped working and was rubbing his eyes.

Hsiang-tung looked at his watch. It was precisely midnight. He took a flashlight out of a drawer in the desk. Lao Fu put on a blue cloth cap and threw a tattered old padded jacket over his shoulders. Then he opened the damper of the stove in the corner of the room and put some water on to boil. He picked up another flashlight and walked out with Hsiang-tung.

"Hm, the weather's changed. The wind's picked up!"

Hsiang-tung never realized that the weather in northern

Kiangsu could change so fast. The moon had set, and the sky had become an expanse of black; and the chill wind was whistling loudly.

The men walked past the two rows of dormitories on the right, and then along the rice paddies. They inspected the animal shed, the threshing grounds, and the barn; then they circled around the broadcasting room, the office, the kitchen, and the dining hall and finally headed back to the duty office.

"All's quiet," Lao Fu remarked lightly, as he hung up his cap and jacket. He began to cook the noodles. In his years of living alone, he had become quite a hand at cooking, and his movements were quick and sure. Hsiang-tung handed him the eggs and noodles, and then just stood by and watched him as he worked.

"You people have been pretty lucky these past three months. You've only lost some meat, a little bit of fish, and a few *mantous*," said Lao Fu, as he prepared the noodles. "The autumn before last, in one night we lost seven bags of rice, each one weighing between one and two hundred catties. That was the worst time. In the morning they discovered the barn door half open and some wheel marks on the ground; that's all they found."

"Do you mean to say," Hsiang-tung gasped in disbelief, "that the thieves used a cart and that more than one person was involved? Did they find out who stole the rice?"

"Find out?" scoffed Lao Fu. "The incident was reported to the County Guard Section, and they sent people over to investigate. And the farm's Party secretary and chief administrator spent the better part of a day with them, but no official report was ever issued. From then on, such incidents always went unreported."

Hsiang-tung was speechless. Thrusting his arms behind his back, he again began pacing beside the table. But Lao Fu quickly produced two bowls of noodles and coaxed him into sitting down to eat with him. Although the ingredients were quite ordinary, Lao Fu's handiwork had produced a very tasty dish. Hsiang-tung insisted on washing the dishes, and by the time he had finished cleaning up, Lao Fu was already cutting out another piece of tin. Hsiang-tung looked at the gray hair on the other man's temples and smothered a sigh. Then he sat down opposite him and opened the book of selections from Lenin.

But he could not concentrate. He read two pages without having the slightest idea of what it was all about. He envied the way Lao Fu was able to concentrate on his work.

"Before . . . " Unable to restrain himself, Hsiang-tung began to question the other man again. "I mean to say, before the Cultural Revolution, what did you do in your spare time?"

Lao Fu looked at him curiously, then glanced at the book in his hands, and said coldly, "I read books."

"Is that so?" Hsiang-tung unconsciously responded in the same tone of voice.

Lao Fu stared at him, then lowered his head and continued with his cutting. After a moment he began to speak again, nonchalantly, as if he were talking about someone else's past. His head remained bent over his work as he talked. "I used to love books. Aside from the books of my trade, I especially loved literature and history. My father had studied literature and left me a great many books. Then since I was an avid book-buyer myself, I collected some eight or nine hundred volumes. At the beginning of the Cultural Revolution, during the tearing down of the "four olds"—old culture, old customs, old habits, and old thoughts—I burned all my old copies of the traditional books. Afterward, as the new writers started to fall, one by one, I didn't have the time to sort them out, so I just borrowed a wooden cart and took the whole lot to the garbage station and sold them as waste paper for four cents a catty. Since then, except for *Mao's Selections*, I haven't bought a single book."

Hsiang-tung couldn't say a word. A picture he had often seen in TV documentaries flashed across his mind: Chairman Mao receiving foreign visitors, and behind him bookcases filled with books, all valuable treasures.

Books, books. He abruptly pushed away the one in front of him and stood up. Tap! Tap! Lao Fu was punching holes again, monotonously, mechanically, endlessly. Hsiang-tung put his arms behind his back once more and again started pacing across the small room. He was so upset that he wanted to stamp his foot with all his might, although he knew it wouldn't help matters. He could only retrace his own footsteps, back and forth, hopelessly.

"Why do I read books?" he suddenly asked himself. If Chairman Mao is the only one left in the entire country who reads and collects books, then what sort of future is there for Chinese culture? And what has the Cultural Revolution done to culture? A whole string of questions crowded his mind, until his head felt like bursting, while his heart felt empty. He stuck his face against the windowpane to cool his hot cheeks and lost all consciousness of place and time.

In the midst of his confusion he seemed to hear a dog barking. He lifted his head. The light, Lao Fu, the kerosene stove—they immediately pulled him back to reality. He was instantly on the alert.

"I heard the cook's dog barking," he said to Lao Fu. "Shall we go and take a look?"

"The dog's barking? All right," Lao Fu agreed unenthusiastically, as he put down his work.

Hsiang-tung picked up the flashlight. "I'll go to the right, you go to the left, and we'll meet at the dining hall."

He opened the door and ran out. The night was dark, and the wind was blowing. He switched on the flashlight and walked briskly toward the dining hall. Except for the sound of his own footsteps, there was a deathly silence all around him. He began to wonder if he had been overly nervous and had mistaken the sound of the wind for a barking dog. He flashed his light on the dining hall door and saw that it was still locked, and as he swept his flashlight past the windows, he could see that they were all tightly closed.

He went around to the kitchen, in the rear. The cook's dog growled softly at the flashlight, but when it recognized Hsiang-tung it began to wag its tail. Hsiang-tung flashed his light on the windows and discovered that one of them was open a crack. At the same moment he heard something heavy hit the ground. He ran to one of the windows and peered inside the kitchen. Yes, the opposite window above the stove was also open. He quickly turned around and ran in that direction, but before he got there a shadowy figure started running toward the vegetable field. There really was a thief! At first Hsiang-tung was startled, then he got angry. Without even thinking, he began to chase the thief, pointing the flashlight at the retreating shadow.

The running figure was very tall, and must have had strong legs. Hsiang-tung clenched his teeth and ran as fast as he could; he seemed to be gaining, but he couldn't catch the man. The thief burst across the vegetable field into the potato patch. At the end of the patch, he slipped and fell into a large ditch. He immediately got back on his feet, but just before he fell, he had looked back, and in the beam of the flashlight Hsiang-tung had recognized his large round face and heavy eyebrows. Hsiang-tung stopped dead in his tracks, almost dropping the flashlight.

He stared straight ahead, into the darkness. The wind began whistling again, blending with the sound of his be-labored breathing. Then he heard the dog barking again. It must be Lao Fu chasing over with the dog. He started to walk back, carefully shining his light on the potato patch, picking his way along the ditch. He met Lao Fu and the dog at the edge of the vegetable field.

"Did you see anything?" asked Lao Fu.

Hsiang-tung shook his head. His heart was beating heavily. "It looked like a black silhouette. I chased it for a while but I didn't see anything."

There was more he wanted to say, but his mouth was too parched. He hoped that Lao Fu wouldn't pursue the matter any further. He was relieved to hear Lao Fu say, "A thief who comes to the kitchen could only be trying to steal some-thing to eat. Let's go. We'd better wake up the cook so he can see if anything's missing."

Residency Check

I DIDN'T KNOW P'ENG YÜ-LIEN VERY WELL. ALTHOUGH WE were close neighbors—my bedroom window faced hers and the front door of her apartment—we had no opportunity to chat because we worked in different units. On those occasions when we did meet on the way to and from work, she always smiled warmly, exposing her white, even teeth and looking at me with moist, glistening eyes. I could not help meeting her glance and answering her smile with one of my own. The old women who lived in the university dormitory called her a siren behind her back, most likely because they were jealous of her captivating eyes.

As far as we women were concerned, Yü-lien was by no means a beauty, and was, in fact, very short. But since she took such good care of herself and was very particular about what she wore, her figure always appeared well proportioned. Her breasts were large and curvaceous, and attracted immediate attention. She always had her hair cut and blown dry at the large hairdresser's near the Drum Tower, and although she wore it in the same bobbed fashion as everyone else, hers was always nicely fluffed, in what the girls called the "Shanghai style." Her skin was dark, her nose was a little flat, and she had a large round face that didn't seem to suit her small stature. But her eyes were big and bright and so expressive that when she looked at you, they held all manner of allurements. Men were captivated by her, so naturally many of the women looked upon her with envy and malice.

The first time I actually talked with her was on a winter morning soon after I moved into the compound. We were pushing our bicycles out our front doors at the same time that day, and we had our shopping baskets hanging from the handlebars. She called out good morning to me, I returned her greeting, and we rode together to the market. The weather was terribly cold, and I was bundled up in a padded jacket, padded trousers, padded shoes, a fur-lined coat, and a snow cap. I was wearing so many layers of clothing that it was a real effort just to get on my bicycle. But P'eng Yü-lien was wearing only a pair of Shanghai-made maroon woolen slip-on shoes with flaps over the insteps; navy blue woolen trousers, a gaily patterned silk padded jacket, closely fitted so as to show off her figure; a maroon woolen cap; and a pair of black gloves. With the snow-covered ground as a setting, she looked particularly lovely and enticing

It takes a lot of nerve to wear such bright colors, I thought.

Our breath was turning to mist, and I commented, "I never thought that Nanking winters would be so cold!"

"I never did like Nanking," she said frankly. "It's freezing cold in the winter and stiflingly hot in the summer. Now Shanghai has a nice climate. If you have a strong constitution you can get through the winter nicely with only a heavy sweater."

I surmised from these exaggerated words of praise that she was from Shanghai. People from Shanghai always seem to have a superiority complex, and to this day the Communist Party has been unable to transform it.

"What a mean bunch they are!" she suddenly blurted out, as she stomped down heavily on the pedal. "They *would* choose a snowy night to come around and make their residency check! Did they check you out last night too?"

"Yes."

I shivered, just thinking about the night before, when I had crawled out of my warm bed to be interrogated, and then got back into a cold bed with icy hands and feet.

"They come to my place every time they have one of their residency checks; their mothers' . . . !"

That was the first time I had ever heard a woman utter this classic curse. I lowered my head and dared not look at her.

I too was fed up with residency checks. There was little anyone could say if they checked every household, but on those occasions when a random check was held, only a few families in each building were picked out. People claimed that anyone who is a problem case is checked every single time. My apartment was one of those that was always checked, but no matter how much I resented it, I didn't dare complain.

"I wonder why they had another random residency check last night," I said.

"What else, except they found themselves with nothing to do after dinner?" she said with a sneer. "According to the people who work in the clock factory, Nixon is on his way to Peking, and public safety measures are being taken everywhere. It would seem that those public safety measures have reached all the way down to us."

By then we had arrived at the marketplace, and since there was such a crowd of people there, neither of us felt like talking any more. We parted company and lined up to buy food.

Following that first meeting, I took special notice of P'eng Yü-lien because of her husband, Leng Tzu-hsüan. They seemed to be a very unlikely couple. First of all, there was a marked disparity in their ages. Although Yü-lien was approaching her middle years, in general appearance and in the way she made herself up, she was holding on to her youth. Her husband gave quite the opposite impression, and seemed to be on the decline. It was said that Leng was not yet fifty, but his face was already deeply furrowed and half his hair had turned gray. He was bald around the temples, and his receding hairline left a broad expanse of forehead. Although he wore glasses, he was so terribly near-sighted that he would hunch his back and thrust his head out whenever he wanted to see something. In sharp contrast to his wife, he hardly ever smiled, and he was so reticent that he shied away from greeting any of his neighbors. The blank, far-away expression on his face always gave me the impression that he had some knotty problem on his mind.

One summer day just before evening fell, I caught a glimpse of him through the window. He was standing outside, leaning against his front door, and looking blankly up into the sky. His mouth was open and he was absolutely motionless, like some kind of fossil. Only when his daughter, who had come out to call him to dinner, tugged at his jacket, did he snap out of it. He lowered his eyes, adjusted his glasses with one hand, and stared at his daughter with a puzzled look.

He was an old man, no question about it, and I felt a little sorry for Yü-lien. But during the first year that I lived in the dormitory I saw Leng Tzu-hsüan only a few times, since he spent most of the time away performing manual labor.

The very day that I moved in the secretary of the Party committee in my department came over especially to acquaint me with the political status of my neighbors. She mentioned Leng Tzu-hsüan again and again, calling him an "old-time rightist." Later I occasionally overheard my fellow teachers refer to him as an "old political target," for he had been attacked in several political campaigns. He had been in detention for over a year in conjunction with the Cleansing of the Class Ranks and had also been found wanting during the recent One Attack, Three Antis campaign. This latest misfortune had come about in a most peculiar manner: One of the teachers—no one knows who—had written "Chinese Communist Party" on a piece of scratch paper, and Leng had added the word "dogs." Someone retrieved the crumpled piece of paper from the wastebasket and forwarded it on up, and as a result one more account had to be settled on top of all the others. Reeducation through labor was ordered, and so an associate professor became a standing member of the May Seventh Cadre school labor force, which kept him away from home from then on.

But the incident that really aroused my interest in P'eng Yü-lien occurred in the summer of 1972. One evening Chou Min, who worked in my department, called on me and asked me to go with her to a meeting of the neighborhood committee. Besides being colleagues, we lived in the same building. I spent quite a bit of time with Chou Min because I liked her kind, gentle ways.

"What kind of meeting is it this time, Hsiao Chou? If it's another planned parenthood meeting, I'm not going. I've already been to several of those, and I've filled out all the required forms."

"No, that's not it," she said with a giggle. "This time it's about the P'an Chin-lien* affair."

"P'an Chin-lien?"

"I'm talking about your *honorable* neighbor, P'eng Yü-lien."

She pointed through my bedroom window, then hurried me along. "Come on, let's go. You'll find out what it's all about when we get to the neighborhood committee meeting."

The meeting was being held in another building, in the apartment of a carpenter named Ch'ang. Since Mrs. Ch'ang didn't work she regularly served as the committee chairwoman, and every time there was a meeting she kicked her

---

*The notorious heroine of the sixteenth-century novel *Chin P'ing Mei*, who was something of a nymphomaniac.

husband out of the apartment.

By the time we arrived the room was already filled with women, and as I looked around I saw that all of the Lengs' neighbors were there; every block representative was in attendance, even tottering old Kuo Nai-nai and Shih Nai-nai. The room was buzzing with their chatter. Chou Min and I found seats on the corner of the bed. I finally realized that they suspected P'eng Yü-lien of having an extramarital affair and were discussing ways of keeping her under surveillance.

"Do they have any proof?" I turned to ask Chou Min.

"Proof?" Shih Nai-nai, who was sitting in front of me, turned around. "We have all kinds of proof! There have been several eyewitnesses. With my own eyes I once saw a man slipping away from her place early in the morning. Pfui! What a piece of trash! Another time someone was seen sneaking into her place in the middle of the night. You just know he had to be up to no good. That shameless hussy doesn't even give a thought to the fact that she has a ten-year-old daughter!"

It came as no surprise that Shih Nai-nai should speak so harshly of P'eng Yü-lien, for she had been widowed as a young woman and had raised two sons by herself. One of them had joined the army and the other was a Party member, so among all the people in our dormitory compound she was the most highly respected. It was only natural that she could not tolerate the slightest moral lapse.

"She is shameless, all right!" seventy-year-old Kuo Nai-nai railed. "While her man is out performing manual labor, she is blatantly carrying on with other men. How will she ever be able to raise a daughter like that? Every time I see her all made up like some kind of demon I just want to throw up!"

"You said it!" Chou Min added critically. "Her outlandish clothing has already been criticized several times, but she'll never learn her lesson and change her ways!"

"Change her ways? Why, she's out there flaunting herself in front of us!" Shih Nai-nai added with considerable spirit. "Do you all remember last summer when she wore that transparent pink silk blouse? She was wearing her brassiere so high that her breasts swayed and jiggled as she swaggered back and forth in the compound. Yen Nai-nai was making some comment about it to her when she cut her short and mumbled that big breasts are for men to suck on. Just imagine saying a thing like that! Poor Yen Nai-nai was so embarrassed she blushed all over and was almost in tears as she walked away."

"Didn't Chairwoman Ch'ang also criticize her clothing once?" A woman who lived next door to P'eng Yü-lien seized the moment to denounce her. "She didn't dare talk back to her face, but the moment the chairwoman stepped out the door, she started to bellow: 'You expect me to start dressing up like a widow before my old man is even dead!' "

Chairwoman Ch'ang's temper flared up. "If we don't straighten her out," she said, "the moral atmosphere of the whole dormitory will be destroyed. And if the young girls follow her lead!" She clapped her hands to get everyone's attention and called the meeting to order.

"Mei Lao-shih,"—I never dreamed that I would be the first person called on—"your place is directly opposite hers. Have you noticed any indiscretions?"

"Indiscretions?" I was caught completely by surprise, and since the place was filled with people, I began to stammer. "I'm . . . not aware of any."

"The reason we asked you here today was to discuss ways of catching her just once," the chairwoman stated. "Your window is exactly opposite hers, which means you can clearly see and hear anything that goes on inside. So we're going to rely on you to keep this area covered."

I felt that I couldn't do that, but I didn't dare refuse. While I was pondering my dilemma, Chou Min poked me in the back, so finally I begrudgingly acquiesced to their request.

"That's fine," the chairwoman said in a louder tone of voice, as she looked over the crowd of people with satisfaction. "That takes care of her front door, and we have Shih Nai-nai and the others to keep an eye out in the rear. Now we have to come up with the specific steps to be taken."

"This is what I would do," said Kuo Nai-nai, who was always very verbal during meetings despite her advanced age. "The moment we see a man entering her house, we must go to the university security section and have them make a search. Then once we've caught her we can hold a big group session and soundly criticize her!"

This met with unanimous approval. Suddenly Chou Min asked, "What if she refuses to open her door?"

"That's right," the chairwoman said, her resolve beginning to waver. "We must have an excuse for going into her house."

"How about a residency check!" someone shouted out.

"Good idea!" several people agreed, applauding.

"Who would dare refuse to open her door for a residency check?"

The plan of action was thus decided: Anyone who saw a man entering P'eng Yü-lien's place was to make an immediate report to the neighborhood committee, which would post sentries at the front and rear. Then they would place a call to the university security section and ask them to send someone to catch the adultress.

At this point the meeting should have come to an end, but since P'eng Yü-lien was such a notorious figure, once we began talking about her we couldn't stop. We all seemed to have forgotten our fatigue after a hard day's work, and we were concerned only that we not miss a single tidbit of news. We craned our necks and cocked our heads as we listened intently. I had never been very clear on the P'eng Yü-lien matter to begin with, and now here I was with the assignment of keeping watch over her. Naturally, in order to gain a true understanding of the person under my surveillance, I sat there from start to finish, taking in every comment, no matter how casual.

I discovered that this wasn't the first time she had gotten into trouble. Back in 1963, during the Four Cleansings campaign,* Leng Tzu-hsüan had gone with his labor group to She Yang county to participate in the Three Togethers movement—eat together, live together, and labor together with members of a commune. Before long, the Party secre-

---

*(Szu-ch'ing yün-tung.) A campaign in which the people and the lower-level cadres were called upon to give a clean account of their political and ideological stand, family background, and financial situation.

tary of his department, Ma Sui, began hanging around P'eng Yü-lien on the pretext that it was his duty to look after the welfare of the members of his department. This Ma Sui was good-looking, fair, and had a real gift of gab, so P'eng Yü-lien soon fell under his spell and into his grasp.

At the time, all her neighbors could see what was going on, but since Ma Sui was, after all, a Party secretary, no one dared breathe a word about it. At first he would just come over for a secret rendezvous and leave after they had had their fun. But as time went on he grew more brazen and would actually spend the night at the Lengs' house when Mrs. Ma was out of town on an assignment. The affair became common knowledge throughout the dormitory district, and even Mrs. Ma got wind of it, though she never let on. The neighbors were incensed by the whole sordid affair, to say the least, but no one had the heart to tell Leng Tzu-hsüan.

After finishing with P'eng Yü-lien, Ma Sui took up with the wife of the boilerman at the school. But they did not handle themselves very discreetly, and they were discovered by the woman's husband. A public uproar followed and Ma Sui was forced to make a formal written statement of self-criticism. The Party secretary of the school did everything within his power to hush up the scandal, but as luck would have it, his efforts were thwarted by the ushering in of the Great Cultural Revolution. The boilerman joined the ranks of the rebels, and his wife came forward to denounce Ma Sui. He was ordered to make a clean breast of things, and when he submitted his confession, there was a resounding outcry. It turned out that he had been involved with a total of five women at the school, mostly teachers, including P'eng Yü-lien; the methods he used and the details of the affairs shocked and disgusted the people.

During the outcry the streets were covered with wall posters criticizing Ma Sui, all the way from the school gate to the cafeteria, and they were pored over by a continuous stream of people. This was the first that Leng knew of the scandal involving his wife, and talk had it that within just a few days half his hair turned white and his walk became a shuffling gait, as though he had aged ten years or more. For the longest time he spoke to no one, and he acted like a mental incompetent. Some people were even afraid that he would try to take his own life.

"Didn't the two of them have a big fight or anything once the scandal was exposed?" I asked Chou Min.

She smiled and said, "That's the strange part about it all. Shih Nai-nai has lived opposite the back door of their place for more than ten years, and she says she's never once heard them have an argument!"

"Really?" This puzzled me too. "But since the whole street was buzzing with the affair, I imagine P'eng Yü-lien had to write a confession, didn't she?"

"A confession?" Shih Nai-nai turned around to break in on our conversation. "Don't even mention that 'confession' of hers! We had one talk after another with her, until our tongues nearly fell out, but all we were able to squeeze out of her was one page. Now I don't know how to read, so I didn't see it, but those who did weren't satisfied with it. You want to know why? Because she wasn't being truthful, that's why! She stubbornly protested that she was being wrongly accused, and that the only reason she had had any dealings with Ma Sui had something to do with removing her husband's rightist label. According to her, falling into his hands had been unavoidable, and she said something about how it would have been harmful to her husband if she had breathed a word to anyone about it. I think she was under the illusion that we would all go out and erect a memorial arch for her or something!"

Carpenter Ch'ang walked in the door as she was saying her piece. We all looked at the clock. It was already past ten, so we quickly brought the discussion to an end and left.

One evening as I was walking home with my son, after picking him up at the day care center after work, I saw P'eng Yü-lien riding her bicycle toward us. She had a large speckled hen in the nylon mesh bag on her handlebars. When she saw us she stopped and jumped to the ground.

"Why didn't you ride your bike today, Mei Lao-shih?" she asked good-naturedly.

"One of my colleagues borrowed it," I answered with a smile.

She had a joyous look on her face, and she was composed, as usual. Her black, shiny eyes, even her dark skin, which was accentuated by her snowy white teeth, were attractive. She was wearing a pair of blue cotton slacks and a white dacron blouse under a lightweight gold sweater. She didn't look all puffy like everyone else, but rather delicate and lively, and everything fit her just perfectly. Not only were the colors of her outfit well chosen, but even the way she wore her clothes was different. In Nanking the women wore sweaters underneath their coats—no one wore them as outer garments. The talk had it that only factory girls from Shanghai dared to do so, and that even in Shanghai they attracted a good deal of attention as they walked along the street. P'eng Yü-lien showed a great deal of nerve in dressing so conspicuously and parading around in the dormitory district of a prestigious university. It was easy to understand why she was looked upon as an immoral person.

The moment my son spotted the chicken his eyes widened and were riveted on it. With a flurry of gestures, he began to shout, "Mommy, a chicken! A chicken!"

Feeling a little embarrassed, I was glad to take a cue from his words. "Where did you get such a big hen?" I asked.

"Someone from the Swallow Hill Commune brought some over to sell near our factory." She smiled again as she spoke. "Three-fifty apiece. I know that's pretty expensive, but it's a fine chicken and well worth it. My philosophy is to eat whenever the food's available. It's better insurance to store things in your stomach than to deposit the money in the bank, as some people do." She laughed, evidently pleased with her witticism. Then, seeing that the child's eyes were still on the chicken, she bent over and asked him, "Your name is Ta-ta, isn't it? Do you like to eat chicken?"

He tugged at my sleeve, "Mommy, I want to eat chicken!"

Before I could say a word, Yü-lien turned to me and asked very seriously, "Would you like one? You can have this one! It's no trouble for me to get them."

"No," I quickly demurred, "no."

"If not now, then perhaps I can get one for you the next time they come around."

I could see by her face that she wasn't making the offer just to be polite. Nonetheless, I momentarily lost my composure. Shaking my head and making signs with my hands, I said, "No! No! I . . . I don't like chicken."

"Really?"

She stared at me incredulously. The smile slowly disappeared, and her face darkened. I avoided her eyes, as I felt my cheeks flush.

"Then let's just forget the whole thing," she said in an obviously forced tone. "So long, then. I'd better be going."

As I watched her ride off I breathed a sigh of relief.

"Hsiao Mei!"

I turned back to see Chou Min, who had come up behind me during all of this.

"What's going on between you and P'eng Yü-lien?"

I told her that we had met on the road and that she had offered to give me the chicken. "She's quite a forthright and ingenuous girl, that one," I concluded aloud.

Chou Min nodded her head. Then in a low voice she said abruptly, "You wouldn't know, but she was once a model worker."

"A model worker?" I could scarcely believe my ears.

"That's the truth!" Chou Min could not keep from smiling. After a moment she took my son's hand, and the three of us walked slowly to the dormitory. On the way she confided to me, "Outside of her fondness for prettying herself up and her extramarital affairs, there's nothing really wrong with Yü-lien. As for her family background, her father was a vegetable farmer in Min-hang village near Shanghai, which makes him a member of the prestigious Five Red Elements.

She joined the Communist Youth League as a young girl, and was on the point of being admitted into the Party when she was dismissed from the League because of her affair with Ma Sui."

"That's pretty severe punishment," I said.

"The Nanking Clock Factory, where she works, took that action only after constant pressure by the rebel faction here at our school. At first they argued that since she had been seduced, the blame should rest with the man, not with the woman."

"Do they know who the man is this time?"

Chou Min shook her head. "According to Shih Nai-nai it's not someone from this area, so most likely he's from the clock factory."

"If they catch him, the people at the clock factory won't have any excuses this time around!"

Chou Min raised her eyebrows and said with a smile, "That's hard to say. The Nanking Clock Factory can't fill the demand for their wristwatches, since they can't meet their production quotas as it is, how could they concern themselves with matters like this? Besides, the problem of relations between the sexes in factories is nothing new, unlike political questions, which can always be expanded and magnified. At most, it's nothing more than a decadent life style, and the worst that can happen is that they have to write out a confession. But that Ma Sui affair was a moral outrage, and the people were incensed over it. They demanded that he be dealt with severely, and the university had no recourse but to report to the provincial authorities and request that he be demoted and take a cut in salary. But their request was denied by the provincial authorities."

"Why was it denied?"

"They said that even though the situation was bad, it couldn't be considered rape, since all the teachers and workers had gotten involved with him of their own free will. They considered it just a matter of life style, which could be dealt with through education. Naturally, the university was put in the bad position of being unable to face up to its own people, so after much negotiating the provincial authorities finally transferred him to another university."

"Really, there doesn't seem to be . . . " I was going to say that there was no such thing as right or wrong anymore, but I held back and said indifferently, "No wonder Yü-lien has done the same thing over and over."

"Hsiao Chou," I said, "don't you get the feeling that P'eng and Leng aren't very well suited to each other? She's still so full of life, and he looks like he's on his last legs."

"He has aged a great deal these last few years," Chou Min said by way of agreement, although there was a sympathetic ring to her words. "You may not believe it, but in the past it was she who chased after him."

"Really!"

Chou Min laughed when she saw how startled I was. But she quickly assumed a more serious air as she continued, "You're not aware of it, but the Leng of the pre–anti-rightist campaign and the Leng of today might just as well be two different people! He was promoted to associate professor in 1967—I remember it distinctly, since that was the very year

I was sent here to teach. At the time his wife had been dead just a year, and he had no plans to remarry. He met Yü-lien quite by chance at the home of one of his colleagues. She fell for him the moment she laid eyes on him, and she took the lead in getting him to go rowing with her at People's Park. In no time at all he was hooked, and the two of them were constantly together. Three months later they were married."

"Incredible!"

"Hai! Naturally, he was a totally different man in those days. He was really full of spirit then. Just think, an associate professor in his early thirties! Why, he walked with such style, with his chest out. People even copied his way of walking! He had been a star pupil at Nanking University—it was called Ginling University then—and a young man of real brilliance. He excelled in everything, including poetry. But he had too high an opinion of himself, and he was awfully naive. During the Hundred Flowers Campaign he took the slogans seriously and really blossomed out with attacks on the cultural and educational policies of the Communist Party and the government. As a result he was the first person in the school to be labeled a rightist element."

"Quite a . . . " I was about to say "typical bookworm," but I couldn't be so unfeeling, and so I just let out a long sigh.

"There was a time when the people in his department entertained the idea of removing that label from him. But just then his department head discovered that he had written a poem that he called 'Snow,' a title that Chairman Mao had used, and had set it in the form of 'Spring in Ch'in Yüan,' just as Mao had done. But the mood of Leng's poem was very dismal and chilling, quite the opposite of Mao's. As far as everyone was concerned, Leng was purposely throwing out a challenge, intending it as a satirical attack on Mao Tse-tung. So not only did he not lose the label, he was lucky he didn't find himself wearing it to the crematorium!"

"Did you see the poem?" My curiosity was aroused.

Chou Min shook her head. "That Leng Tzu-hsüan isn't one to back down. Even though he wrote several confessions, he insisted that he had only written what he saw and felt, and he steadfastly denied that any satire had been intended. Some people demanded that the whole poem be made public, but the department authorities weren't willing to have this unhealthy influence spread any further, so they kept it classified, together with his written confession. The entire department hotly criticized and discussed the affair for a while, even though hardly anyone knew the actual contents of the poisonous weed!"

By this time we had passed through the main gate of the compound, and, probably because we were within range of the eyes and ears of others, Chou Min said nothing more on the subject. We said goodbye and each of us headed home.

One night soon after that my dreams were suddenly shattered by the sound of someone knocking on a door. I awoke and strained my ears. Sure enough, someone was knocking on the Lengs' door. That Yü-lien is sure a sound sleeper, I thought; the noise woke me but there wasn't a peep from her. Then I heard a man shout impatiently, "Open up in there! Residency check!"

Another residency check! Just hearing the words disgusted me, as I knew that there would be no more sleep for me the rest of the night. Being nervous and a poor sleeper by nature, I found it next to impossible to close my eyes again if I awoke during the night. Since the residency check was sure to include my place, I figured I might just as well get up and wait for them so I wouldn't be flustered at the last minute, and also to prevent my son from waking.

I turned on the light, got dressed, dug out my residence documents, and sat in front of my desk by the window to wait. Just then the clock on the wall began chiming the hour—it was midnight, a typical hour for a residency check. I lifted a corner of the curtain to look outside. It was pitch black except for a light coming from the Leng apartment. Their front door was ajar, and I could see someone moving behind the window, but because of the curtain separating us, I couldn't see clearly. I let my curtain fall back into place, and began to flip through a book.

As I had expected, in about the time it would take to drink a cup of tea, someone came knocking at my door. I walked over leisurely, opened the door, and with the same motion handed over my residence documents.

"Oh, pardon us, we're not here for a residency check." At this I became uneasy. The first person through the door turned out to be Mrs. Ch'ang, the chairwoman of the neighborhood committee. There was an unwonted look of apology on her face. She was followed by two men who belonged to the school security section and a woman whose face seemed familiar to me—most likely she was a member of one of the school workers' families.

"Here's why we've come," Chairwoman Ch'ang was saying. "We suspect that P'eng Yü-lien is up to something.

Earlier this evening someone saw a man sneak into her house and did not see him come out. Just a while ago we entered her place on the pretext of a residency check but we didn't find a man inside. Yü-lien was red in the face, like a thief who's been caught in the act, but since she hadn't violated any law, we couldn't very well make her open up her trunks and cabinets so we could look through them. We think she hid him somewhere, so we've come to ask you to keep an eye on her and to be sure to report anything suspicious to the neighborhood committee."

There was nothing I could do but assent, and after a few more admonitions by the chairwoman, the four of them departed.

As if I had nothing better to do than meddle in things like this! Anger filled my heart as I undressed, turned off the light, and got back into bed.

But just as I had feared, after this ordeal, any chance of going back to sleep had vanished. I just tossed and turned in bed, and like someone who has drunk a lot of strong tea, I grew more and more wakeful. That damned P'eng Yü-lien! After all that tossing about in bed I couldn't keep from cursing her. Everyone in the neighborhood had to lie awake nights because she got herself into trouble! But then I thought of how she had been in imminent danger of being disgraced in front of everyone, and I ended up by being glad for her. But just who was the man? Here I was, living directly opposite her, and I had never noticed an unfamiliar man entering or leaving her house. In a big dormitory like this, I thought to myself, with all these people living close together, there naturally were many tongues to wag. Who knows?

Some gossip may have raised a false alarm, which started the people talking and gave rise to a groundless disturbance.

After giving rein to my thoughts for a while—I had no idea what time it was—I noticed the faint light of day coming in through the window, and then the shape of the window itself gradually became visible. Since sleep was out of the question, I decided to get up and get dressed, make myself some tea, and then amuse myself by writing in my diary.

I happened to pull back a corner of the curtain and glance out the window. Imagine my shock when I saw the Lengs' front door open slightly and without a sound. Then a head peeked out through the opening and looked left and right. It was followed stealthily by the rest of the body. With lowered head and hat pulled low, the figure tiptoed toward the rear gate of the compound. In my agitation I didn't get a good look at the person's face, but there could be no doubt that it was a man—I wasn't mistaken about that. The Lengs' door was already closed when I looked back; there were no lights in the house and the curtain was pulled down all the way. Suddenly one corner of the curtain was raised, and someone's face was pressed against the glass. The instant our eyes met we both withdrew and lowered the curtains as quickly as possible.

I remained standing beside the window for a long time, my legs rubbery, my hands clasped tightly together and pressed against my breast, as I tried to stop my heart from beating so wildly. If I live a hundred years, I'll never forget P'eng Yü-lien's wide staring eyes. Was her look one of terror, mortification, or defiance? I shall never know.

Before the day was out, news of the P'eng Yü-lien affair had spread throughout the school and the dormitory. By sheer coincidence, Chou Min had risen early that morning and noticed a man with his hat pulled down over his eyes. She saw him walk very nervously toward the rear gate, open it with a key, and leave. When Chairwoman Ch'ang came over in the morning for information, Hsiao Chou reported what she had seen. Actually, she hadn't seen which house he had come out of, but everyone eagerly jumped to the conclusion that he was none other than P'eng Yü-lien's lover. People said that the chairwoman recalled seeing a key lying on a table while the neighborhood committee members were making their residency check the night before. She surmised that P'eng Yü-lien had hidden the man in the wardrobe, but in the excitement she hadn't had time to hide the key. Once Chairwoman Ch'ang figured this out she stamped her foot and yelled, "What a shame!" But there was nothing to be gained by regret, and since they hadn't caught the culprit, naturally they had no case against P'eng Yü-lien. She continued to ride her bicycle around the dormitory area in complete freedom, like someone without a care in the world.

The news inevitably reached the May Seventh farm in northern Kiangsu. The farm closed down for a few days before New Year's, and on the eve of Leng's departure for Nanking, his section leader called him in and told him about the affair. He advised him that if he wanted a divorce, the school authorities would be willing to consider his request since P'eng Yü-lien had repeated her offense time and again.

But to everyone's surprise, Leng stated without any show

of emotion, "If Yü-lien wants a divorce, I'll consent to it any time, but under no circumstances will I bring up the subject myself."

This bit of news became *the* topic of conversation. Some expressed wonderment and admiration for his "magnanimity," while others called him a spineless weakling who would not let go of a "worn-out shoe." Then there were those who gleefully predicted that it would be strange indeed if he didn't beat her within an inch of her life the moment the two of them were together!

But as it turned out, on the day that Leng arrived home, Yü-lien, her face beaming with joy, brought home an old hen, and as she plucked its feathers she was even humming to herself. Her neighbors kept their ears pricked all night, waiting for the sounds of an argument that never came. At this point the school notified Leng that he was to teach a language course, so he no longer had to take part in manual labor. From then on I saw him often; sometimes he would be walking all alone in the schoolyard, while at other times he would be sitting next to the window in his quarters, lost in thought and looking up into the sky for hours on end. On my way to and from work I also ran into Yü-lien quite often, and she greeted me with a smile as always, but she never again stopped to chat.

Jen Hsiu-lan

In the summer of 1971 Nanking had plenty of rain, so the grass and shrubbery were exceptionally lush. As the supervisor of the Elementary Students Management Section, one of my main responsibilities was to supervise the children as they tended the lawn in front of our office.

I was one of three women teachers from the Hydraulic Engineering College who were in charge of over thirty children. Their parents—teachers and staff members of the school—were undergoing labor reform in northern Kiangsu in accordance with the May Seventh Directive, and as there were no grandparents in the families to look after the children, they were left in our care. Even with a relatively small number of children, we still had to take possession of six classrooms to house them and provide for their school work and their recreational needs. The row of rooms faced south, and the large plot of grass in front of it became our responsibility. Several heavy downpours since the beginning of summer made the grass grow very fast, and I had been chosen to see that the children cut the lawn every weekend.

One Saturday morning in early August as the children and I were working in front of the building as usual, several of the fifth- and sixth-grade boys slipped away to play on Ch'ing-liang Hill, above us. The younger children continued to work cheerfully, talking and laughing as they weeded and cut the grass, some using their hands and others using scythes. By high noon everyone was soaked with perspiration, but the work was finished and everything was neat and clean. Just as we were putting our tools away, Ma Shih-fu* of the Workers' Publicity Corps came running toward us, waving at me, oblivious of the sweat pouring down his face.

When I saw how upset he was my heart leapt into my mouth, for I was afraid that the boys who had slipped off to the hill had gotten into some kind of trouble. Once before, when a student had fallen out of a tree while reaching for a bird's egg, Ma Shih-fu had rushed to inform me in exactly the same manner.

"Ma Shih-fu!" I hurried forward to meet him.

"Ch'en Lao-shih, I've got to see you!" was all he said as he hurried toward our office.

I told the children to go wash their hands for lunch, all except the Wang sisters, whom I asked to dispose of the grass clippings. Then I anxiously rushed over to the office. Ma Shih-fu was nervously pacing back and forth. The minute I entered the room he shut the door.

---

*Shih-fu is a polite term for an artisan or laborer.

"Jen Hsiu-lan has run away!" he said abruptly, fiercely scratching the back of his head. He was very upset and seemed at a loss for what to do.

"Jen Hsiu-lan run away?"

No wonder he was so upset. Jen Hsiu-lan was a former Party secretary of our school. She had been a fanatic "leftist" at the beginning of the Cultural Revolution, but she was now under detention in a "study class" after being indicted as a leader of the May Sixteenth counterrevolutionary group.* Her husband was a political secretary of one of the divisions of the Nanking Military District and had been a well-known policy maker when the rebels first rose to power during the Cultural Revolution. However, when the present campaign began he was among the first group of people detained in the military district study classes. Among other crimes, his wife had been accused of acting as a liaison between the military and the university; she was said to be the local extension of the black arm of the Nanking military counterrevolutionaries. It was, of course, a very serious matter if such a person ran away.

"Yes, she's gone!" Ma Shih-fu exclaimed as though he had been personally victimized; his wrinkled old face lengthened with anger. "It happened before eight o'clock this morning. She fooled us, saying that she was going to the toilet, then she just disappeared!"

But how could she have run away? The target of each

---

*(*Wu-i-liu fan-ko-ming chi-tuan.*) An ultra-leftist group that was said to be particularly opposed to Premier Chou En-lai and the Ministry of Foreign Affairs. Leaders of this group were said to be important lieutenants of Chiang Ch'ing during the Cultural Revolution.

study class was constantly surrounded by five or six people who "studied" together day and night, slept in the same room, ate together, and even went to the toilet together. Moreover, the windows of all the rooms were encased with wooden bars. With such close security, it was nearly impossible for her to escape, and of all places, from the toilet! Jen Hsiu-lan's ingenuity was indeed almost supernatural, I thought.

"Wasn't the window of the toilet nailed shut?" I asked.

"Aiya! I don't know when, but she loosened two of the wooden bars by pulling out the nails! Those guards are good for nothing but stuffing themselves with rice. God damn it!" Ma Shih-fu began to curse.

We were used to hearing curses from the members of the Workers' Publicity Corps, even from such a kindly old man as Ma. He had previously been a janitor in the Nanking Chemical Fiber Factory, but after being assigned to the Hydraulic Engineering College, he became as important as the Military Publicity Corps members. But even with his high position he was always modest and good-natured, never putting on airs. At the meetings he would often bow to the people and say, "I've come to learn from you." He was the only member of the Workers' Publicity Corps who was well thought of by one and all. The pity was that because he was illiterate and had no education, he was qualified only to manage production development. Our Elementary Students Management Corps was under his supervision, and teachers Yü, Hsia, and I got along very well with him, often asking for his advice.

"Jen Hsiu-lan can't possibly get very far," I comforted

him. "They're out to get all the May Sixteenth rebels, so she really has no place to hide."

"That's hard to say," he shook his head uncertainly. "There are too many May Sixteenth rebels in hiding. She didn't have her purse with her, so without money and ration cards she'll need help. After all, a rabbit can't grow a long tail!"

When I heard that Jen Hsiu-lan had no ration cards I really began to worry about her. "Have you searched Ch'ing-liang Hill?" I asked.

"Of course, right away. But there wasn't a trace of her! That's why I've come looking for you. The hill is so large and so thick with trees and tall grass that several people could easily hide there. We just had a meeting and decided to have the students go up and search the hill."

That really took me by surprise. To take thirty or so children of various ages up to search the hill was a big responsibility. But then, how could I refuse the assignment? "No problem," I said, keeping my face expressionless.

Ma Shih-fu nodded apologetically. "I really shouldn't bother you three teachers, since you all have nursing babies at home, but we're short-handed. With over twenty study classes going on in the school, and Jen Hsiu-lan running away, it's impossible to get anyone, especially since we've got to be doubly on our guard. We've also got to keep this a secret, because if the news were to reach the May Sixteenth confederates, there might be trouble."

He scratched his head again, and sighed deeply. "We're really desperately short of help. Every available person has already been assigned a job. Not only do we have to search

up and down every street, but we've also got to send people
to watch the train station and the docks. The whole school
has been mobilized, and everyone in the Military Publicity
Corps has come out to join in the search. I think our Management Division should do its share, and since the children
have nothing to do, let them look among the trees and in the
tall grass. Maybe they'll find something before dark."

We agreed that we would wait until the children had
finished their lunch. Then he would join us in going up the
hill.

When the children heard that they were going to search
the hill for a runaway they were very excited. Little Ming,
the leader among the boys, immediately found some sticks
to distribute among the bigger boys. The Wang sisters, not
to be outdone, went to the dining hall and wheedled the
cook into giving them some sticks for the girls too. Everyone
in the school knew about Jen Hsiu-lan, and there was a
certain element of precocious seriousness in the children's
excitement; even the first-graders behaved as though they
were about to confront the enemy and talked to one another
in whispers.

As soon as Ma Shih-fu arrived, the children rushed toward
the hill like a swarm of bees, each of them struggling to be
the first to get there.

"Form a line! Form a line!" Ma shouted hoarsely. "Proceed just like combing hair—don't miss a single spot! If you
find anything, report it immediately."

With Ma Shih-fu at the eastern end and me at the western end, and the children between us, we formed an uneven
twisting human line that slowly made its way up the hill.

The Hydraulic Engineering College had been built on the side of Ch'ing-liang Hill and, together with the Nanking Crematorium, occupied half the hillside. Aside from the Military Division based at Tiger Pass, the rest of the hill was uninhabited, but since many people came to get firewood and farmers cut the grass to feed their animals, the area was not completely wild. That day, as we swept up the hill, the guards posted by the Liberation Army had been alerted to expect us, but several old men who were cutting grass watched us as we bent over and turned aside nearly every blade of grass. "What are you looking for?" they asked.

"We lost some money!" the children answered in unison.

"Money?" The old men squinted at Ma Shih-fu and me in obvious disbelief. However, they asked no more questions, and before long they gathered their things and left silently.

The Wang sisters were walking beside me, chattering incessantly, and as they searched through the grass, I overheard them discussing a girl named Shih Hung, who seemed to be related to Jen Hsiu-lan.

"Who's Shih Hung?" I asked.

"She's Jen Hsiu-lan's daughter."

I had heard that Jen Hsiu-lan's youngest daughter was a middle school student and had been a Red Guard leader. She was exceedingly active and quite well known. My curiosity aroused, I asked, "Do you know her?"

"Our oldest sister's her classmate!" the older one boasted. "She used to come to school in a jeep! But now she walks like a shadow and doesn't talk to anyone."

"Our oldest sister's teacher said that everyone must watch her because she might commit suicide!"

Suicide! It was terribly unsettling to see a fifth-grade child talk of suicide without batting an eye.

"Even if her parents are May Sixteenth elements," I exclaimed, "it's got nothing to do with her as long as she takes a clear stand."

"They wanted her to denounce her parents, but she insists they are not May Sixteenth elements, and she won't back down. Our sister and her other classmates have even pasted up wall posters criticizing her."

She certainly is a worthy daughter of Jen Hsiu-lan, I thought to myself. She's absolutely unyielding.

One of the Wang girls interrupted her searching to ask me solemnly, "Ch'en Lao-shih, Jen Hsiu-lan is a May Sixteenth element, isn't she?"

"Um"—I wasn't at all sure about this myself—"probably so. Both the Workers' Publicity Division and the Military Publicity Division publicly declared that she was, and they can't be wrong, can they?"

I was ashamed to give the child such an indefinite answer, but, in truth, I was very confused about the May Sixteenth incident. In 1967, when I was in Peking, I heard about a May Sixteenth Rebel Army Unit that had posted the slogan, "Aim a cannon at Premier Chou" in Tienanmen Square. It had been removed almost immediately. Soon afterward, Chiang Ch'ing herself exposed several counterrevolutionary organizations, among which the May Sixteenth Rebel Army Unit was mentioned. But again this had all been hushed up and in time forgotten. No one could have foreseen that after a few years, when the One Attack and Three Antis campaign was in full swing, the denouncement of the May Sixteenth group would resurface on orders from above. The May Sixteenth group was declared a left extremist organization, a bold and vicious gang of people who had dared to oppose Mao Tse-tung, openly attacked Chang Ch'un-ch'iao in Shanghai, and pointed a finger at Hsü Shih-you in Nanking. General Hsü, vowing that he would "defend Mao Tse-tung's ideology to the death," swept through the military and the universities, eliminating the gang's members with a great hue and cry.

The people of Nanking had been unaware of the existence of this group. It was only after the upheaval that they realized that it was this terrorist gang that had been behind all the murders, looting, and destruction during the Cultural Revolution. Nanking was described as the main base of the May Sixteenth group, from which its influence had infiltrated the army and slowly spread throughout the whole nation. Since Nanking is an important base of the Liberation Army, it was necessary to purge the city thoroughly of this evil.

As the purge got under way many people were arrested in the military units, in the factories, and in the universities. Terror was rampant. According to an announcement by the Military Publicity Corps of the Hydraulic Engineering College, the number of May Sixteenth elements in our school was in three digits, which meant that there were at least 100 and possibly as many as 999. Since there were only 1,000 or so in the entire school, people began to look suspiciously at one another, wondering if everyone else was a counterrevolutionary.

Nanking University had been a model for all the colleges

in Nanking, and that was no less true during this campaign. I still remember vividly the first May Sixteenth Confession Meeting sponsored by the university. It was a hot day, and the sun shone fiercely on the more than 20,000 people sitting in the huge, heavily guarded athletic field. One by one the May Sixteenth elements were forced up onto a high platform, where they were publicly accused. They then confessed amid tears and hysterical sobbing, some of them even fainting on the stage. Among the offenders was one who had been collecting incorrect sayings of Mao Tse-tung with the intention of using them for the "usurpation of power" when the time was right. There was a Red Guard who had taken a copy of Hitler's *Mein Kampf* while ransacking the library, and after studying the book thoroughly, he had made it his personal bible. There were also some who had been classmates for years, sharing the same quarters, and even some couples who had been married for over thirty years, who were completely unaware of each other's membership in this dreaded gang. The audience was badly shaken; I personally was absolutely dazed.

Was Jen Hsiu-lan a member of the May Sixteenth gang? I really did not know—only Heaven knows.

We continued our search until dark, up and down the hill, without discovering anything suspicious. The children figured that Jen Hsiu-lan had already fled from Ch'ing-liang Hill. Everyone was exhausted, and some of the smaller girls kept leaning against me. Ma Shih-fu decided to call it a day, so we headed back with the children.

The next morning, before we teachers could begin our daily study of the *Selected Writings of Chairman Mao*, Ma came running up to us. By this time Jen Hsiu-lan had been gone for more than twenty-four hours. It was assumed that she had had sufficient time to leave Nanking, so the provincial government had telegraphed the security bureaus in her hometown in Shansi province and her husband's hometown of Soochow to put all her relatives under surveillance. Our college also sent people to watch the docks along both sides of the Yangtze River in case she tried to board a boat. The school authorities were afraid that her disappearance had been planned with both inside and outside help, so they intensified security measures to prevent any further such happenings. Ma Shih-fu came to tell us that we must be especially careful to check out Ch'ing-liang Hill every day. "If you notice anything suspicious phone the office immediately." With this instruction, he rushed off.

"What a lot of commotion," Hsia Lao-shih exclaimed as she watched his retreating figure. "Jen Hsiu-lan's disappearance has turned the school upside down. Look at the state Ma Shih-fu's in! He probably didn't get much sleep—his eyes are all bloodshot."

"Dr. Ku is the one to be sorry for," Yü Lao-shih declared. "She was so upset she didn't even go home last night!"

"Why Dr. Ku?" Dr. Ku was a close neighbor of mine, but I wasn't aware that she had been assigned to guard Jen Hsiu-lan.

"That was changed just this summer," Yü Lao-shih informed me. "Jen Hsiu-lan has high blood pressure, but they suspected that she was just putting on an act when she constantly complained of headaches and dizziness. Sometimes there wouldn't be a sound out of her for a whole day and

night, and even thunder wouldn't have shaken her. They
didn't know what to do, and they weren't sure whether her
illness was real or feigned, so they finally reported the situation. The Workers' Publicity Corps said that this was easy
to handle: all they had to do was assign a physician to be her
guard and find out if she was pretending to be ill or not. So
they put Dr. Ku in charge. Who would have thought that she
would be the one to land in trouble!"

I felt badly for the doctor, who was a good person, gentle
and kind.

"There were so many guards around her," I protested,
"that they can't possibly put all the blame on Dr. Ku."

Hsia Lao-shih, who seemed to derive pleasure from seeing
someone else in trouble, asked, "Well, why did she allow it
to happen while she was on duty? She and Chou were on
night duty, and after they got up in the morning Chou went
to the dining hall to get breakfast. While she was making
her bed, Jen Hsiu-lan was given permission to go to the toilet
and just never came back. When Chou returned with breakfast they discovered she was gone. Naturally, the responsibility was mostly Dr. Ku's."

"By coincidence, Dr. Ku once belonged to the Revolutionary Red Liaison group that Jen Hsiu-lan supported, so
this puts her in a very difficult position," Yü Lao-shih added
somewhat sympathetically. "Jen Hsiu-lan couldn't possibly
have loosened the nails from two wooden bars in a single day
and night. They suspect that she had been working on them
for several months with her hairpin. The guards simply
hadn't suspected a thing."

"She's really fast!" I said. "After climbing out of the

toilet window and running across the yard, she still had to make her way around the laboratory before she could go up Ch'ing-liang Hill. At most, she had only ten minutes."

Jen Hsiu-lan had been locked up in one of two small buildings on a little hill on the western side of the campus. These buildings had once been occupied by the Workers' Publicity Corps when they first came to our school. Because they proclaimed that they were the true Marxist-Leninist representatives, who were spreading the thoughts of Mao Tse-tung, the place had come to be called Marx-Lenin Hill. It could not be considered an isolated area, as it stood next to the Hydraulic Engineering building and in front of the laboratory. It was very unlikely that anyone could have run up to Ch'ing-liang Hill without being seen.

"You see, she's been a guerrilla ever since she was a child. She's known as the 'long-legged general,' " said Hsia Lao-shih.

"She's really something!" Yü Lao-shih shook her head with a sigh, though there was an overtone of admiration. "She's been an old cadre member since the days in northern Shansi, and she's had plenty of experience in purging others. So although she's the one being purged now, it won't be easy to knock her down. She's probably the only woman ever appointed as Party secretary to a university in Nanking."

"She's an old fox!" Hsia Lao-shih said. "At the beginning of the Cultural Revolution she sided with one group while attacking another, purging many rebel groups in the process. Now when the call is 'cadres step to the side' she's the first to fall. As far as I'm concerned, she's getting what's coming to her!"

Yü Lao-shih gave me a meaningful look, and it suddenly dawned on me that Hsia had once belonged to a rebel group that had been attacked by Jen Hsiu-lan. No wonder she was so gratified by all this trouble. Every day we heard the slogan "eliminate factionalism," yet the roots of the different groups formed during the Cultural Revolution went too deep.

"You weren't here at the college when Jen Hsiu-lan was at the peak of her fame, were you?" Yü Lao-shih asked me, changing the subject.

I shook my head. Although Jen Hsiu-lan was a notorious figure, I had seen her only a few times, and then only very briefly. The first time was when she passed by with a labor reform group, leading those still "unliberated" black elements in shouldering hoes on their way to work. A colleague had quietly pointed her out: "That older woman with the touch of gray in her hair is Jen Hsiu-lan. She used to be a real sharpshooter; can you imagine that? In the old days she fought all over the T'ai-hang Mountains. She joined the guerrillas when she was only fourteen and the Party at sixteen." I had looked at the short, stocky figure with increased admiration.

I saw her for the last time in the spring, when our school, following Nanking University's example, called for a May Sixteenth Confession Meeting. It was attended by the whole school. All the May Sixteenth suspects were brought in; Jen Hsiu-lan, the last to enter, was seated in the front row. I remember the way she walked in: calm, her head held high, her lips curled slightly in the semblance of a smile as her eyes slowly swept the hall with an unfaltering gaze. I imagined that must have been how she looked when she used to mount the stage to make reports to the whole school. But this time she looked much older; her face, no longer round, was wrinkled, and her hair was considerably grayer. She was also much thinner, unlike the others, who had grown plump and pale from a lack of sunshine and exercise.

"Jen Hsiu-lan really used to have style," Yü Lao-shih reminisced. "She often worked with us, wearing patched cloth shoes and a faded blue uniform. When we stopped for a rest she'd munch on a *mantou* without even washing her hands. I was deeply impressed until the Wang sisters' mother told me that her oldest daughter had been to Jen Hsiu-lan's home—a large Western-style house with leather sofas and carpets on the floor, where even tea was served by an aide. So her simple austerity was just a show, put on for our benefit!"

I was about to express my feelings when Hsia Lao-shih hastily interjected, "Two-faced! Typically two-faced!"

Ignoring her, Yü Lao-shih continued, "At one time Jen Hsiu-lan advocated 'saving the country through physical fitness.' She organized ball games and a *t'ai-chi* boxing class for the female staff of the school, which I joined. You know, although she was short and plump, she was pretty good! She'd finish a whole set of boxing in five minutes without puffing or getting all red in the face. Once we had a race and we all dropped out halfway through; all except for her, that is—she was the only one who finished a lap around the athletic field. She's really got strong legs. So I think that ten minutes would be enough for her to make her escape."

Talk of the race reminded me of what we were supposed to be doing. "The school has asked us to intensify our patrolling," I said, "so we'd better hurry and make some plans."

Hsia Lao-shih shook her head in disagreement. "I think it's useless. We've already been through all of Ch'ing-liang Hill like a comb several times. She must be out of Nanking by now. The minute they discovered she was missing yesterday they organized groups to search the hill and the laboratory, and the Publicity Section personally conducted a search of Marx-Lenin Hill. They turned over every blade of grass and went through the house where she'd been imprisoned, inside and out. They even opened up the cesspool outside the toilet and prodded it with a stick! I think she's already gone to Shanghai, where the black line of the May Sixteenth gang is stretched far and wide. Even worse, she may have joined our nation's enemies!"

In spite of all these speculations, we still carried out our instructions. We took turns leading the children up the hill daily, and we shook the trees and beat the grass. After a few days the children began to forget what they were there for, and most of them simply threw away their sticks and ran off to play. Finally, only the younger ones were left to return with the teachers.

By Friday afternoon nothing had been accomplished. The school was very quiet since almost everyone had been sent out on assignments. After seeing the children finish their dinner, I turned my duties over to Yü Lao-shih and dragged myself wearily back to the dormitory. Halfway there I met Dr. Ku. It had only been a few days since I had last seen her, but she was much thinner. Her eyes were sunken, her face was waxen and yellow, and she looked haggard.

"Dr. Ku!" I greeted her warmly, running up to grasp her hand tightly in sympathy.

"Ch'en Lao-shih!" She placed her other hand over mine, looking at me with grateful eyes, which reddened even before she began to speak: "I really have rotten luck!"

"Don't worry, they'll find her," I said in a low voice. "They can't put the blame entirely on you; it's difficult to guard against this sort of thing."

She looked up and down the road to see if anyone was around. "I'm really unlucky. I've been here only two months, and already this has happened. By the time I came they'd already stopped following her to the toilet—that didn't start with me. Jen Hsiu-lan is very cunning. She'd been shut up for over a year, but during these last few months she'd been on her best behavior. She didn't play any tricks, such as fasting or pretending to be ill, and every day she'd study Chairman Mao's selected works before concentrating on her own writing. Everyone was relieved and began to relax. Who could have known she had secret plans! Aiya, what'll I do?"

I wanted to comfort her some more, but she shook her head and pressed my hand tightly. "I've got to go to a meeting," she said, and walked off with her head bowed. My heart pained as I turned to watch her small, thin figure. At that moment I truly hoped that Jen Hsiu-lan would be found soon.

The next day was Saturday again. Just as I was about to organize the children for some gardening, Ma Shih-fu walked up.

"Ch'en Lao-shih, let's start all over again. We'll find her."

He tried to sound optimistic but he couldn't hide his low spirits. "We had an emergency meeting last night. The reports have come in from everywhere—still no news. They believe that Jen Hsiu-lan is probably still in Nanking, possibly hiding in the western or southern part of the city, so they've directed us to begin the search all over again. This time we'll split up into separate groups and go over the grounds inch by inch. We'll dig into every hole and leave no stone unturned. The most important part is Ch'ing-liang Hill and the homes around that area—they'll be searched by the Military Publicity Corps. You'll take charge of Marx-Lenin Hill. Begin right away, and I'll come and help as soon as I finish giving the other groups their assignments." He then gave me two keys and left.

With the imprisonment of Jen Hsiu-lan on Marx-Lenin Hill, the place had been declared off-limits to the children. So they were excited when they heard that they were to search there and went hunting for sticks again. I divided them into two groups: four or five older girls would search the inside of the house with me, while all the other children would search the grounds around it. Actually, no one had any hopes of finding a trace of Jen Hsiu-lan, but the children were so curious about Marx-Lenin Hill that they could not even wait to form an orderly line. They dashed off up the hill the minute I gave the order to go.

I took the Wang sisters and several other girls inside the four-room house where Jen Hsiu-lan had stayed. Three of the rooms were furnished with tables, chairs, and benches. Two of them had evidently been used by the guards for their meetings, as the walls were covered with portraits of Mao

Tse-tung and various rousing slogans such as "We Shall Not Give Up until the May Sixteenth Gang is Vanquished!" "Pluck Out the Military Black Hand That Has Extended into Our School!" "Whoever Opposes General Hsü Opposes Chairman Mao!" The third room must have been where Jen Hsiu-lan's thought-reform sessions had taken place, since the walls were all covered with huge black characters and six-inch-long exclamation marks. The slogans exhorted her to "Bow Your Head and Confess!" and "Turn Back to the Shore!" One read "Even in Death There Is No Place to Hide!"

The fourth room had served as a bedroom for Jen Hsiu-lan and her night guard. It had two windows but they were covered with black curtains. The room was so dark and gloomy that the girls were afraid to enter until I drew back the curtains, letting in the bright August sun. As in all the other rooms, five or six wooden bars had been nailed across the outside of the windows.

There were two wooden beds in the room. One was bare, while the other, probably Jen Hsiu-lan's, still had a pillow and a quilt on it. Under the bed were two pair of shoes—one black leather, the other of quilted cotton. There was also a loose bedroll, which had obviously been searched many times. Several suits of ordinary cloth uniforms were piled on the two chairs between the beds, and a very old copy of Chairman Mao's selected writings was on the desk. The plaster walls showed scraps of recently removed posters, apparently torn down in such haste that some characters were still partly legible: "Dead-End," "Where to?" and the like.

We lingered awhile, touching this and that even though

there weren't many things to be searched through. The children were disappointed, and got down on their hands and knees and looked carefully under the beds.

"Shall we take a look at the toilet, Lao-shih?" one of the Wang sisters asked me.

"Yes, why don't we?" It took us a while before we found it, at the end of the veranda. I opened the door and went in first. Just then we heard loud shouts from the children outside the toilet window.

"Ch'en Lao-shih! Hurry! Ch'en Lao-shih!"

I dashed out, colliding with a child who was rushing inside at the same moment.

"Hurry, Ch'en Lao-shih, hurry!" It was little Ming who grabbed my hand and pulled me around the corner of the house to a spot beneath the toilet window. The children were gathered in a tight circle, staring wide-eyed at something. Some of them were covering their noses, while several of the younger ones were hiding behind the others, their hands over their faces in fright. They quickly moved back to let me get a closer look. What I saw was the three-foot-square cesspool solidly filled with some object.

"Jen Hsiu-lan!"

I don't know who called out the name, but the instant I heard it I became violently ill; a bolt of light flashed before me and I blacked out. I neither heard nor saw anything more.

I was sick for a whole week, I lay in bed not wanting to eat or drink, and every time I closed my eyes a black mass would float into my mind and I would become nauseated. Gradually I got better, and I realized that my reaction was not a physical one. A strong emotional chain was wrapped around my heart, and I would never in my life be able to unlock it.

Ma Shih-fu was very concerned about me and came to see me several times. He told me about the large criticism meeting that was held at the school. Many people had mounted the stage to denounce Jen Hsiu-lan, declaring that she "began by pretending to be a leftist" and "ended by being an extreme rightist," that she "destroyed herself in the face of the people," and that her death "carried less weight than a feather." Naturally, her name would "stink down through the centuries." She was posthumously expelled from the Party and officially labeled a counterrevolutionary.

"If she wanted to kill herself by jumping into a cesspool, what could we do?" Even Ma Shih-fu sighed as he shook his head ruefully. "Just think, that cesspool is rather shallow— only about three feet deep—and not even as long as a person's body. If she hadn't squeezed into the corner, we would have found her the first time we poked around in it. Ai! Why seek death? Dying like this is . . . how did they say it at the meeting? Oh, yes, 'carried less weight . . . less weight than a feather!' "

He was right.

That autumn the Lin Piao incident occurred,* and very soon it was full steam ahead with "Criticize Lin" and "Attack extreme rightists." Before a year had passed, all the May Sixteenth elements who had confessed publicly on the stages had recanted their confessions, claiming they had been co-

---

*The alleged coup by Mao's right-hand man, and his subsequent death during an escape attempt.

erced by torture and beatings. Many of their accusers were imprisoned and put into study classes as suspected Lin Piao followers. The alleged May Sixteenth elements in our school were gradually released—the last one being freed after three years of incarceration—and declared innocent of all charges.

The wheel of class struggle rolled on, and very soon May Sixteenth became a historical note in Nanking, a memory of terror touched with absurdity. No one mentioned the death of Jen Hsiu-lan any more, her name appearing only on the historical record of struggles at the Hydraulic Engineering College.

But for me it is different. Her death has been like an iron weight in my heart, sinking ever deeper.

The Big Fish

K'UAI SHIH-FU CAME HOME EARLY ONE FEBRUARY DAY. HE popped his head inside the door and asked his wife, who was lying in bed, "How are you feeling? Any better?"

Mama K'uai had turned her head at the sound of the door opening, and now her face lit up at the unexpected pleasure of seeing her husband. She didn't wish to worry him so she answered evasively, "Seems better. Doesn't hurt so much."

The windows and doors were tightly shut against the bitter cold, with wads of newspaper stuffed into the cracks. The odor of Chinese herbal medicine permeated the room.

"Have you taken your medicine?" K'uai Shih-fu asked as he glanced at the earthen pot on the small round table beside the bed.

"Yes, Chang Sao prepared it. She even cooked lunch for me."

Mama K'uai's voice was filled with gratitude, even though the person who had done all these favors was not present. Her old backaches had recurred, and for the past few days she had spent most of her time in bed. Without their neighbors' help, K'uai Shih-fu wouldn't have been able to go to work.

"Why are you home so early?" asked Mama K'uai, looking at the old clock on the wall near the foot of the bed. It was only three o'clock.

K'uai Shih-fu worked at the dockyards, some distance away. His work and his meetings usually kept him busy from morning to night, and since he had to change buses to get from the Yangtze River Bridge to Cock Crow Temple, he never got home before dark.

"This afternoon we were supposed to have political study, but they said some American newspapermen were coming to Nanking, so at the last minute it was changed to a general clean-up. Those two apprentices of mine are really very thoughtful. They know you're sick and they wouldn't let me do anything. They practically forced me to go home."

As he talked, the old man took off his gloves and poured himself a glass of hot water from the thermos bottle on top of the chest of drawers. He cupped his hands around the glass for warmth.

Mama K'uai smiled. "Those two young fellows seem to be all right. Let's just hope they won't turn out like the last one, who cursed you as though you weren't worth a cent as soon as the Cultural Revolution began!"

The old man grinned as he sat down by the small round table. He blew on the glass of hot water before taking a tentative sip; he found that it was not too hot and gulped it all down.

"What else could he have done under the circumstances?" he asked without resentment. "The campaign was in full swing and he had to take a radical stand if he didn't want to get in trouble himself. He felt sorry about it afterward, and he used to come when no one was around to apologize for what he did. At the time he thought about nothing but the revolution, so he neglected his work entirely. Now whenever he is in difficulty, doesn't he always come running to me?"

"That's because you're so good-hearted!" Mama K'uai laughed. She was able to accept the incident now, but two years earlier, when she had learned that the old man's apprentice had attacked him in wall posters, she had been very upset. Especially disturbing was the fiasco of inviting the apprentice over for dinner one New Year's eve. It was entirely her idea, but the apprentice accused the old man of having ulterior motives, of going the way of the "imperialists," trying to "cultivate" and "corrupt" young workers. When the old man was subsequently forced onto the stage for "confession and criticism," the old woman seethed with anger.

"Speaking of my apprentices, I almost forgot!" the old man exclaimed. "They said that during the welcome for the American newspapermen, for the next couple of days the markets will be better stocked than usual, especially the one on Tung Jen Street. They said you can get anything you want, so tell me what you feel like eating and I'll go out and get it for you."

The old woman closed her eyes and thought it over. Since

she had not been to market for over a week, her husband had had to pick up what he could on his way home from work, and they had eaten nothing but frozen cabbage for some time. It had been cabbage with soy sauce one day and cabbage with salt pork the next. The old woman was bothered by a bad stomach to begin with, and the monotony of the diet had robbed her of what little appetite she had left.

"I could go for a taste of fish soup," she said, her eyes brightening at the prospect. "It would be nice if you could get a fish. Just think how delicious it would be, cooked with a few slices of ginger and some scallions. We could add a little bit of rice wine just before we eat it!"

That was enough to make the old man's mouth water. "You want to eat fish? All right, you shall have it!"

He stood up and straightened his cotton-padded cap, which he had not even removed after entering the house. Then he patted the pocket of his quilted jacket to make sure his money was there.

"I'll go to the Tung Jen Street market right away. My apprentices said they've got everything there!"

He went into the kitchen, took a look at the stove, and was pleased to see a circle of blue flame underneath. He opened the bottom door a slit wider to get a little more ventilation, and picked up the market basket.

K'uai Shih-fu considered the distance between Cock Crow Temple and Tung Jen Street and decided to go by bicycle. It took him some time to get his bicycle out from under the bed, where it was stored. The tires were flat, of course, so he had to find the pump and inflate them. After all this effort the old man was breathing hard, but the thought of the fish he was going to bring home made him jubilant. His wife was every bit as elated as he as she watched him bustling about.

"I'm leaving," he called as he pushed the bicycle out the door.

"Hurry back," she said. "If you can manage to buy a fish, that'll be just grand."

K'uai Shih-fu turned out of the small lane onto Cock Crow Temple Road, which led all the way to the south gate of People's Park and was always crowded. Accustomed as he was to lining up for the bus before daybreak, K'uai Shih-fu rode his bicycle with a great feeling of freedom and exhilaration. As he wove in and out among the pedestrians, the hoarse sound of the bell was music to his ears. When he turned onto the wider and more congested Peking Avenue, trucks began whizzing past him one after another as they sped toward Drum Tower Circle. The old man had always dreaded traffic at the circle, so he took a short cut through a small alley and quickly reached Tung Jen Street.

It had been a long time since his last visit to the market. In fact, it had been over a year, when his son came home on leave from the Northeast, and K'uai Shih-fu had gotten up very early one morning to buy a chicken.

The market on Tung Jen Street and the Central Market on New Market Square were both well known. The Municipal Revolutionary Committee looked upon them as places of importance, so they were excellently managed and always well stocked with a wide assortment of fish, meat, and vegetables. Although a good many people came from far away to shop there, the K'uais were not among them. Most of the people who patronized these two markets were Liberation Army personnel and the servants of families of high-level Party members who lived in the area. They spent their money freely, and Mama K'uai, who had always lived a frugal life, disapproved of their ways.

The first thing K'uai Shih-fu noticed was that the entire street had been renovated since his last visit. The grounds had been swept clean and the walls had been washed; and the newly posted political slogans were particularly attractive. Whether they were selling soy sauce, pickled vegetables, groceries, brooms, or toilet paper, the shops on both sides of the street looked as though they had all been carefully rearranged. The windows shone, and even the door fronts had been scrubbed until the bricks were bright red.

K'uai Shih-fu parked his bicycle at the entrance to the marketplace and walked in with his basket. The spotless cement floor had obviously just been washed, so that as he walked K'uai Shih-fu looked back guiltily at the footprints his large cotton-padded shoes had made. There weren't many customers in the market, but there were enough so that every stall had some business. All the stall keepers were wearing freshly washed and starched white knee-length aprons, while those selling meat and fish even had white cotton caps on their heads.

Of all the places in the market, K'uai Shih-fu liked the fish stall the best. The shiny tile counter made the various kinds of fish on display particularly attractive. From a distance, he could see the ribbon-fish and bream that covered the stand. But he could also see that there was a line of people waiting. Just as he was about to get in line, he spotted some other fish on the counter. He stepped forward and saw several large *ch'ing* fish,* all shiny and fresh-looking, laid out in a row.

"Why buy bream when there is *ch'ing* fish?" he thought. Bream has a muddy taste that no amount of seasoning can get rid of.

He saw a stall keeper busily weighing fish, calling out the weights as his free hand clicked the abacus. Another man was squatting in a corner sorting fish from a big wooden box, throwing the large ones into one basket and the small ones into another. K'uai Shih-fu tried to catch the second man's attention. He called out, "Are these *ch'ing* fish for sale?"

The man looked up, frowning at him for some time before answering, "They're out on the stand, so of course they're for sale."

"Then weigh me half a fish!" As he spoke he placed his basket beside the stand, trying to make up his mind which half of the fish he should buy. Mama K'uai had said she wanted some fish soup, and the fish head would make a tastier soup than a chicken! So he had better buy the top half.

"Give me the top half, with the head."

"Can't sell half a fish," the stall keeper answered, shaking his head as he went back to his sorting. "If you want it, you'll have to take the whole fish!"

The old man hesitated. Buy the whole fish? He looked at the price—sixty-five cents a catty. A whole fish would come

---

*A flat gray freshwater fish, popular in central China for making soup.

to two or three dollars.* His hand instinctively moved up to the pocket of his quilted jacket.

"Well?" the man asked, raising his head again. Seeing the look of indecision on K'uai's face, he added coldly, "Each one weighs about four or five catties."

The stall keeper's attitude annoyed K'uai. He patted the top part of his jacket where his month's pay, which he had just received, lay hidden in his inner pocket.

"Okay, go ahead and weigh the whole fish!" he answered briskly.

This caught the man by surprise. Giving K'uai a hard look, he got up slowly and, without saying a word, picked up a large fish and put it on the hook of the steelyard.

"Oh, I'd like that one," K'uai Shih-fu hastily pointed to a smaller fish.

"What's the matter?" The stall keeper pretended not to understand. Lifting the steelyard higher, he swung the dangling fish in front of his customer's face so that the tail nearly brushed against K'uai's chin.

The old man took a step backward and waved his hand in a conciliatory gesture. "Go ahead and weigh it." He'd better not make a fuss, he decided. He consoled himself with the thought that it was a rare opportunity to get such good fish, even though it meant that he and his wife would have to eat fish for the next three days. Luckily the weather was cold, and the fish would not spoil.

"Sixty-five cents . . . four catties and a half . . . that comes

---

*Here "dollars" refers to "renminbi" or "people currency." One dollar renminbi equals a little more than half a U.S. dollar.

to $2.93." The stall keeper blinked his eyes and announced the price without bothering to use his abacus.

K'uai quickly took a five dollar bill from his inner pocket. The man gave him his change and carefully placed the fish in the basket. After another curious look at K'uai Shih-fu, he went back to sorting fish.

The old man let out a deep sigh, but he picked up his market basket and left the fish stall with a feeling of satisfaction. Those young fellows were right, he thought. This Tung Jen Street market was quite a place; a person could actually buy a large *ch'ing* fish here. He was sure his wife wouldn't believe her eyes when she saw the size of the fish. Absorbed in his own sense of accomplishment and grinning happily, he did not notice the curious looks the other customers were giving him. Some of them were even pointing at his basket.

As he passed a vegetable stand, K'uai Shih-fu's eyes lit up. At the end of February produce was always scarce, and he would never have thought that there could be so many kinds of vegetables on display. In addition to the turnips, carrots, and frozen cabbages that were usually available, there were also tomatoes and cucumbers—things he had not seen for a long time. These delicacies were attractively displayed in separate little baskets placed at the most conspicuous spots in the stand. He looked at the price of the tomatoes—fifty cents a catty. He shook his head. They were intentionally priced out of the common people's reach, he thought. In the summer they were only five cents a catty. There was no price on the cucumbers, but since his wife had always been fond of them, he decided to get one, whatever the cost, just so she could eat some fresh vegetables. After being ill for several days, she would enjoy the taste of something different.

"How much are the cucumbers?" he asked a woman vendor.

"The cucumbers are not for sale!" she answered bluntly, her eyes fixed on the fish in his basket.

The old man was disappointed, but since there was nothing he could do, he looked around to see what he could get to cook with the fish head.

"Hurry! Hurry! There are people in line behind you!" The woman gestured impatiently with the steelyard, sending the lead weight and bronze plate clanging against each other.

Under this pressure, K'uai Shih-fu lost his composure and couldn't make up his mind. All of a sudden he remembered that they might be out of ginger at home. "Give me a half a catty of tender ginger." Then he spotted a small basket of bamboo shoots in a corner. He knew that bamboo shoots were very expensive, but they would be delicious cooked with the fish head. He thought of how frugal his wife had been through the years, and decided that she deserved at least one good meal now that she was ill. Bamboo shoots cooked with the fish head—he had not indulged in such luxury in years. "Give me two bamboo shoots." This time he did not even bother to ask the price.

"Sixty-five cents a catty," the woman announced. She emptied the ginger into his basket and went over to weigh the bamboo shoots.

After paying for the vegetables, K'uai Shih-fu picked up the market basket. Feeling its weight, he decided not to buy anything else, but to go straight home and cook the fish. Countless varieties of dishes were displayed in the glass showcases on the prepared food counter, but he gave them only a cursory glance as he hurried toward the main entrance.

More people were coming to shop now. Housewives, laborers coming from work, cadremen, and soldiers in neat uniforms were pouring into the market. He walked over to the place where he had parked his bicycle, which was now just one among many.

"Comrade, is there any more of that fish left?" A man who brushed by him turned back to ask anxiously.

"Yes!" he assured the man enthusiastically. "Hurry, there are still several . . . " Before he had finished speaking, a housewife carrying a basket hurried up to him and broke in, "Comrade, how much is this fish selling for? Is there a long line?"

"No need to stand in line. It's sixty-five cents a catty."

After all the attention his market basket had attracted, K'uai Shih-fu took another look at the large *ch'ing* fish. With its clear bulging eyes and bright scales, it was very impressive looking indeed. The old man's heart was filled with joy.

He carefully hung the market basket on the handlebar of his bicycle. Because of the crowd, he had to push the bicycle out to Tung Jen Street. But when he was about to get on his bicycle, someone tapped him on the shoulder.

"Hey, comrade, take that fish back."

The old man lowered his right leg to the ground and turned to see a middle-aged man with small protruding eyes. From his manner and dress, the old man could tell he was a cadre member.

"What did you say?" He thought the man had mistaken him for someone else.

"That fish isn't for sale," the man said in a low voice,

trying to be patient. "Take it back to the cashier's office immediately, and they'll refund you what you paid for it."

"What?" K'uai raised his voice. "Not for sale? Damn it! Then why the hell didn't they say so in the first place? Now you want to snatch it away when it's about to be dropped in the pot!"

At the old man's curses the cadreman's face hardened and he glared at K'uai.

"If they're all sold out, what'll be left to show the foreign visitors when they arrive?"

K'uai Shih-fu wanted to say something more to give vent to his grievance, but when he heard the words "foreign visitors" he stopped short. The issue was closed. He gulped, then blinked his eyes in stony silence.

The cadreman, seeing that K'uai was not responding, demanded, "What unit do you belong to?"

His insolent tone of voice angered K'uai Shih-fu, who blurted out, "Nanking Dockyard, ironworker for thirty years!" To save himself from further questioning, he gave his type of work and the length of time he had served.

The cadreman softened when he heard that K'uai was an old worker. "Never mind," he said, nodding his head. "You didn't know. Just take the fish back, and the cashier's office will . . . "

"If you want the fish," the old man broke in, "you take it! I'm not going to!"

He recalled the hard looks the man at the fish stall had given him. Now if he were to take the fish back, not only the stall keeper but all the people in the market would stare at him.

A crowd had gathered by this time, looking curiously at the two men. The cadreman was afraid the matter might get out of hand, so he backed down. "I'll take it back for you," he said, "Wait here. I'll bring the money back right away."

Without waiting for an answer, he thrust his hand into the basket and grabbed the fish. With everyone's eyes riveted on him, he walked into the market, holding the fish by the gills.

K'uai Shih-fu looked on helplessly as the fish, its huge tail swinging back and forth, disappeared into the distance. He looked into the basket again. It was empty except for a few pieces of ginger root and two withered bamboo shoots. He could go back and try to buy a bream, but it would probably be all sold out by now. Then as he thought of the long lines, his legs felt weak.

What would he say to Mama K'uai when he got home? That was the most difficult part. She would be even more disappointed if she found out just how close she had come to feasting on that fish. It would probably be best to tell her a lie. In all their years of marriage, K'uai had never lied to his wife.

As he stood there, dazed, a bystander came up and said to him, "You don't seem to know the ropes, do you? Before the foreign visitors have come to look, they won't sell any of the good things. We're all waiting until the foreigners have come and gone before we try to buy any of the specials."

"You can buy them before the foreign visitors arrive," someone said sarcastically with a knowing air. "The only trouble is that you have to take them back. Last time, when Prince Sihanouk came to Nanking, they even brought in turkeys from somewhere. One of my neighbors, who had never seen a turkey, bought one out of curiosity. But he only got it as far as the rear gate before it was sent back. They said they started with five turkeys, and after two days of brisk sales, there were still five turkeys left!"

K'uai Shih-fu couldn't bear to listen any longer. He turned abruptly, and with a backward kick of his right leg, mounted his bicycle.

"Comrade, he hasn't given you back your money!"

"Tell him to give it to the foreign visitors!"

Keng Erh in Peking

ALTHOUGH CLOSING EARLY ON SATURDAYS WAS NOT STIPU-
lated anywhere, by tacit understanding everyone began wrap-
ping things up soon after three, and promptly at four they
left the office, one after the other. For Keng Erh this day
was like all others: Precisely at four o'clock he walked out of
the Research Institute of Mechanics, climbed onto his old
English racing bicycle, and, without first stopping off at his
dormitory, rode out through the gate of the Academy of
Sciences and headed straight for the city. In the western
suburbs of Peking in early November the sky is clear and the
air is crisp, cool without being cold. Keng Erh shifted into
third gear. Whipping along like the wind and chasing after
his own shadow with the afternoon sun at his back, he felt
elated, putting all the tedium and monotony of the past
week out of his mind.

The traffic grew more congested after he passed through the West Gate area, forcing him to slow down. But since he was so familiar with this stretch of road that he could have negotiated it with his eyes closed, he soon arrived at the northern gate of the East Wind Market at Wang Fu Ching. As he parked his bicycle at the stand he saw a line of people stretched all the way to the parking lot waiting for numbers. A bad sign, he thought; he wouldn't have a chance of getting a number. But in spite of that, he ran over and got on the end of the line. What everyone was eagerly awaiting were the fire pots* served by a specialty restaurant. Each day only forty pots were prepared and forty numbers distributed. The first twenty were served from five-thirty to seven o'clock, and the other half from seven on. Since there simply was not enough to go around, people who had a special liking for the mutton fire pot, which was the restaurant's specialty, sometimes started lining up at the foot of the stairs at three in the afternoon.

It was as Keng Erh had anticipated. Before long there was a stir in front of the line as the last number was given out, and the people began to disperse, not without some grumbling. Keng Erh drew close to the foot of the stairs and waited patiently for those who had been given the last twenty numbers to clear away.

"Mr. Keng!"

Lao Lu, the employee responsible for parceling out the numbers, was waving to him from the top of the stairs. Keng

---

*A ring-shaped pot that fits over a charcoal stove and slips down around its chimney. The pot is filled with broth in which the customer cooks thinly sliced meat and vegetables to his own taste.

Erh was so pleased that he dashed up the stairs, two and three steps at a time. Lao Lu unobtrusively placed a small piece of greasy cardboard in his hand. He looked gratefully at Lao Lu, walked into the restaurant, and found a seat by the window.

He placed the ticket on the table in front of him. He felt a little guilty when he saw that it was number eleven. Only that morning during the political study session, besides the criticisms of Lin Piao and Confucius, the discussion had touched on ways of stopping the evil practice of getting things through the back door. Keng Erh was the last one to speak, making an impassioned statement. One of his colleagues was taking minutes, and tried frantically to get it down completely. But did he truly feel guilty? A helpless shrug was his only answer. Everyone shouted and carried on about closing off back doors, yet in private his colleagues invariably discussed how they could find such back doors for themselves. Since Keng Erh lived all alone and his needs were few, he had managed to refrain from this evil practice.

Naturally, eating mutton fire pot was an exception.

This particular back door had been opened to him quite naturally. Ever since the renovation of the East Wind Market and the opening of this restaurant, Keng Erh had been a regular customer. Nearly every week, on Saturday or Sunday, he would have a meal of mutton fire pot, and so he became friendly with Lao Lu. The old Peking Moslem was about ten years older than Keng Erh. His hair was nearly all gray, but his teeth were still white and even, and he cordially flashed them for the benefit of his customers. Neither man knew the other's full name, and at first they had simply called each other Lao Lu and Lao Keng. When Lu learned that Keng Erh worked in the Academy of Sciences, he became very respectful and began calling him Mr. Keng. This filled Keng Erh with regret, but it was too late to do anything about it. He was glad he had not told him that he was a returned overseas scholar and that he had lived in America for twenty years. That would have made matters even worse.

Lao Lu knew that Keng Erh was a bachelor and could appreciate his coming into the city from such a distance in order to eat a meal. So on weekends Lu often took it upon himself to hold back one of the numbers for Keng Erh. Such consideration was not easy to come by, so Keng Erh came even more often.

A young waiter brought a bowl and a pair of chopsticks to his table, and Keng Erh ordered several dishes of sliced beef and mutton, plus some bean-flour noodles, cabbage, and some thin baked wheat cakes. When the waiter had added up the check, Keng Erh handed him a bill and his ration card, and then put the receipt under his bowl. While the people around him were busily ordering food and paying their checks, he reached into the pocket of his Mao jacket and took out a small vial of alcohol and two wads of cotton. Holding his chopsticks under the table, he wiped them off with the cotton balls, then did the same with his bowl.

Ever since several of his colleagues had come down with hepatitis, supposedly from eating in restaurants, he had been on the alert. One of his colleagues had told him about this method of disinfecting eating utensils, but he always felt a bit guilty about it and was especially afraid that Lao Lu might see him.

"Is there anyone else at this table?" a nattily dressed old man smilingly asked Keng Erh. He shook his head, and surreptitiously dropped the cotton balls on the floor. The old man placed his numbered ticket on the table, removed his wool cap and hung it on the wall along with his cane, and very leisurely sat himself down opposite Keng Erh. I must look like a doddering old man myself, Keng Erh thought as he smothered a sigh, since only old people in their seventies and eighties are willing to share a table with me. The thought reminded him of his own age. For a moment he was unable to say just exactly *how* old he was; then he quietly calculated to himself: 1974, 1925 . . . he was precisely forty-nine. Ah, forty-nine! The thought was like a gulp of ice water that left a cold track all the way to the bottom of his heart. The number nine was some sort of milestone in his life: at twenty-nine he received his Ph.D., at thirty-nine he returned to China, and now he was forty-nine. Ten years already! He was single and alone when he returned, and he was still single and alone.

"Is something wrong?" the old man asked solicitously. His hair was white, his face kindly, his expression refined yet friendly.

"No, it's nothing . . . " Keng Erh knew he had forgotten himself and had somehow betrayed his inner feelings, and now he felt embarrassed.

"Nice weather we're having; just the time to be eating mutton fire pot," the old man said, tactfully changing the subject.

Just then Lao Lu appeared with a large round tray. Keng Erh welcomed his presence and called out warmly, "Lao Lu, how's everything these days?"

"Just fine, just fine!" Lao Lu answered crisply. He put down the tray, removed from it eight or nine dishes of sliced meat and vegetables, and laid them out on the table in front of Keng Erh.

"Is there any news from your son?"

"Still the same!" Lao Lu said with a sigh. "I've always said that that boy was born without any luck, but his mother wouldn't believe it. See for yourself. He and his classmates were sent to resettle in Inner Mongolia, and all those who are sons and daughters of cadre members have been recalled and admitted to universities. A fellow who joined his group only last year is now studying English in the Institute of Foreign Languages. I asked him why he couldn't be more like that Chang T'ieh-sheng, who dashed off an anti-establishment letter and had himself sent to Liao-ning Agricultural College."

Lao Lu was so concerned with giving vent to his feelings that he gave no thought to his being overheard. But his complaint was a common one and attracted no attention.

"Well, he's still young. There'll be other opportunities," Keng Erh said in an attempt to console him.

"He's already twenty-five and his old man still has to send him food and clothing. And if his mother wants to see him, the only way he can get home is for us to send him travel money."

Having unburdened himself, Lao Lu suddenly bent over and whispered to Keng Erh, "How about you? Any good news to report?"

Keng Erh shook his head. Lao Lu gave him a comforting

pat on the shoulder, then picked up the other man's ticket and walked away.

Keng Erh and the old man picked up their bowls and went over to get the sauces and spices, and by the time they returned, the old man's dishes had been placed on the table. The waiter threw the change on the table and walked away.

"Hey, comrade, I still have a plate of bean-flour noodles coming." The old man tried to catch the attention of his waiter, but he kept on walking as if he were deaf.

"What an attitude!" The old man shook his head and smiled wryly as he sat down with an air of resignation.

"Forget it, comrade," Keng Erh said as he pushed his own bowl of noodles over. "I have more here than I need."

Just as the old man was about to push it back, Lao Lu walked up with Keng Erh's fire pot. As he lifted the lid, the air was filled with steam.

"Thank you. Thank you very much!" Keng Erh said appreciatively.

The old man took the opportunity to tell the old waiter about the bean-flour noodles.

"Okay, okay! I'll bring some right away," Lao Lu promised as he took a white towel from his shoulder and mopped his brow. Then he turned to Keng Erh. "Eat it while it's hot. Would you like me to get you a glass of Bamboo Green Wine?"*

"I can't let you do that, Lao Lu; I'll get it myself."

Keng Erh hastily got to his feet. Getting wine for the

---

*A strong sweet wine.

customers wasn't the waiters' job, and Lao Lu, especially, was so busy that his face was covered with perspiration. By this time all the tables were filled with customers, some of whom were getting impatient and were waving and shouting for their fire pots.

"The Anti-Lin Piao, Anti-Confucius campaign ought to be winding down now, Mr. Keng," the old waiter whispered into his ear as he accompanied him over to the wine counter. "We're now in a period of policy implementation, so you ought to take advantage of the relaxed atmosphere to have one of your colleagues introduce you to a prospective wife."

Keng Erh said nothing. He simply shook his head and smiled as Lao Lu gave him another consoling pat on the shoulder and walked toward the kitchen.

What a warm friend! Keng Erh was genuinely moved. But such things are more easily said than done. As a matter of fact, getting him married was a matter of considerable interest in his office. His chief and his colleagues had expressed their concern, but where was a man of his years to find a suitable spouse? Back in 1968 there was a young colleague—a conspicuous member of the rebel faction—who said to him, "If you hadn't studied in America, a man of your caliber would long since have had a family!"

He was right on the mark. In those days the status of repatriated Chinese was quite low, especially those who came from America. In the eyes of the rebels, they were either secret agents or incorrigible capitalists. Keng Erh knew that behind his back his colleagues already considered him the "major problem case" in the institute.

Keng Erh brought two glasses of wine back to the table,

then raised his chopsticks to invite the old man to share his meal with him. "You needn't stand on ceremony; go ahead and eat," the old man said, acknowledging this polite gesture.

Just then the other fire pot arrived, and the old man went to the wine counter and bought a large glass of red grape wine. With great ceremony he raised his glass and toasted Keng Erh, who returned the toast. As Keng Erh closed his eyes and savored the sweet taste of the wine, he thought of Hsiao Ch'ing, for it was she who had introduced him to this delicious wine.

"So you like Bamboo Green," the old man remarked as he put down his own glass. "I can't drink it; it's got a more potent after-effect than *kaoliang* wine."*

"It doesn't bother me," Keng Erh replied. "It's sweet, but it has a slight medicinal taste. A friend of mine introduced me to it with mutton fire pot, and I just got used to it. I always have it with mutton fire pot."

"Oh, so that's how it is." The old man nodded, seeming to understand. "I used to like only *shao-hsing* wine myself, and my wife liked grape wine. But ever since she passed away I've taken to drinking grape wine."

"Is that so?" said Keng Erh sympathetically.

Hsiao Ch'ing, he thought, lives in Peking, but as far as he was concerned, she might as well not exist. He could almost see her standing before him, with her dark, moist eyes and her long braids. The wine suddenly seemed to freeze into beads of ice, cold and hard, beating relentlessly against his heart. After the interminable Cultural Revolution had

---

*A potent wine made of sorghum.

passed, the memories of his aborted love affair faded into the past, but he was left with a taste very much like that of Bamboo Green—sweet with a trace of bitterness.

He remembered well his first drink of Bamboo Green, at a restaurant in the western part of the city. Hsiao Ch'ing had received her 1965 year-end bonus and invited him to eat mutton fire pot in celebration of the lunar new year.

"If you don't learn to appreciate mutton fire pot you might as well not live in Peking," she said. "Don't be fooled by the crowds in restaurants that specialize in Peking duck. They are actually for visitors from the provinces. Old-time Peking people don't go in for it much."

Keng Erh had been born and raised in Shanghai, and in his home they never ate mutton. During his years in America he always disliked the smell of stewed lamb. But he readily fell in with Hsiao Ch'ing's suggestion and was surprised to find how delicious it was. He was intrigued by the way it was prepared and served; it was much better than roast duck, all oozing with fat.

The Chinese like to talk about "predestination," and although Keng Erh was no longer a believer, he had not doubted it at all when he first met Hsiao Ch'ing. How else could he explain his finding her in a city as big as Peking? If he hadn't ventured out on his bicycle in the bitter cold weather following the snows in early 1965 to browse through the bookstores, wouldn't he have missed the chance of meeting her? He was grateful also to the New China Bookstore for displaying its dictionaries on a high shelf, for that was the stroke of luck that led to a soft, melodious voice asking him, "Would you mind handing me a copy of the *Concise English-Chinese Dictionary?*"

He turned in the direction of the voice, and there she was. Those eyes of hers, shielded by long eyelashes, were so bright and crystal clear that they reminded him of a glacial lake in the Rockies that he had visited in the United States—so bright that it had made him dizzy and so still that it had seemed removed from this world.

"Are you a student?" It was the only thing he could think to ask as he handed her the book; he was afraid that he might never again see those star-like eyes of hers.

"No, I'm a worker at the Third Textile Mill," she said with candor and pride.

She then told him that the workers were encouraged to study a foreign language, and that she had signed up for the English class. Discovering that she was a local girl, Keng Erh asked her where he could find second-hand bookstores. She told him that the best one was located in the Bridge of Heaven district, an amusement center in southern Peking, and, seeing that he was unfamiliar with the city, she decided to accompany him there. Since she had also come by bicycle, they rode together over to the Bridge of Heaven.

"Hsiao Ch'ing." He could not keep from whispering her name now as he took a sip of wine.

All twenty of the fire pots in the restaurant were now open, and clouds of steam filled the room. Glasses and plates covered the tables, and there was lively conversation everywhere. Keng Erh noticed that the old man's glass was empty and that his once pale face was now suffused with a red glow;

he was at the moment unbuttoning his wool overcoat with slightly trembling hands and breathing through his mouth.

The image of Hsiao Ch'ing's father and the hearty way he drank wine suddenly popped into Keng Erh's mind. The first time he called on her family, the father asked him to stay for dinner and sent her younger brother out to buy some prepared dishes. Then he brought out a bottle of Bamboo Green that he had been hoarding for more than six months. The father would tilt his head back to allow each swallow of wine to course down his throat. Then he would reach out with his chopsticks, pick up three slices of tripe, and put them in his mouth. He was so natural, so completely without affectation. He told Keng Erh a great many things about life in Peking before Liberation, and recalled his experiences as a porter at the railroad station. Warmed by the wine, he even removed his overcoat and fanned himself with a folded newspaper. He was feeling quite merry by the time they finished the bottle. He warmly patted Keng Erh on the back and began to sing in a loud voice—fashionable revolutionary songs as well as some obscure melodies.

What a lovable old man! And Hsiao Ch'ing was just like him in temperament. Keng Erh had never met a girl who was so frank and open, so artless—a simple, sincere, and completely natural girl. Except for her large eyes and long lashes, she looked nothing like the girl of his dreams: her skin was not fair, she was not tall, and she was not a college student. What's more, she was nineteen years younger than he. And yet she exerted a mysterious force upon him, drawing him to her like a magnet and holding him tightly against her. From the moment of their first meeting, Keng Erh no longer felt rootless and alone, as he had during all his years as a drifter in a strange land. When he was with her not only was he ineffably happy but he also felt safe and secure. With the release of all his suppressed emotions, there was no need to struggle to keep up appearances. He felt he had reverted to the innocence of childhood. Hsiao Ch'ing loved to laugh, and her laugh was so cheerful, so bright, and so warm that it brought spring and sunshine wherever she went.

After parting at the Bridge of Heaven he went at once to a store and bought himself a second-hand Shanghai bicycle in good condition. Then he returned to his dormitory and put away his English racer. How flashy and conspicuous his new foreign bicycle had appeared alongside her old domestic bicycle! Soon after their first meeting Hsiao Ch'ing found out that he had studied abroad, but she didn't hold that against him at all, unlike so many of his colleagues who called him "The Yankee" behind his back, making him feel like a steer that has been branded with an indelible mark.

Hsiao Ch'ing was a model worker of New China. She was filled with pride and dignity but she was also capable of maintaining an attitude toward foreign things that was neither superior nor obsequious. In this she differed from many of Keng Erh's younger colleagues at the institute, who generally disparaged anything and everything foreign on principle, but on occasion betrayed a blind admiration for such things. In point of fact, she was full of curiosity for anything new. On those occasions when Ken Erh mentioned the history of some foreign nation or some wonder of nature he had seen, she listened with wide-eyed curiosity and rapt attention. Sometimes she would ask him endless questions, wanting desperately to get to the bottom of everything. She worked even harder at her English, now that Keng Erh was her teacher. In the summer of that year the two of them often went to the rear hill of the Summer Palace to study. It was much quieter there among the trees than on the shores of K'unming Lake, which attracted most of the tourists.

Keng Erh never tried to conceal his feelings, although he never expressed them in words either, for fear that the pressure on Hsiao Ch'ing would be too great. At the time she was only twenty years old, a whole generation younger than he, and he knew that it was up to him to control himself. He would have to proceed slowly and not force himself on her. His love could not be like the white heat of the noonday sun, its rays shining everywhere; instead he had to pattern himself after the setting sun, warm without scorching. But the tenderness and affection in the depths of his heart were like the lava in an underground volcano, which seethed and flowed in search of the opportunity to explode to the surface. Hsiao Ch'ing was somewhat hesitant at first—Keng Erh assumed that she was troubled by the differences between them in nearly every respect—but as summer approached she gradually warmed to him, even taking it upon herself to change her day off at the mill to Sunday so that they could be together. When she saw a co-worker with whom she was friendly she would cheerfully call out to her and then introduce Keng Erh.

"Mr. Keng, here, have some candy." Lao Lu broke in on his thoughts.

"What's the happy occasion?" Keng Erh asked as he laid down his chopsticks and picked up the three pieces of soft candy Lao Lu had placed in front of him.

"Our chief cook got married today and treated us all."
Lao Lu had a big grin on his face, as though he himself were
getting married. He had brought a pot of hot water to refill
the two fire pots on the table. "Don't forget, now, I expect
to be repaid three-fold when you pass out your own wedding
candy." With that, he turned around to pour hot water at
another table.

"You can count on it," Keng Erh assured him as he put
the candy in his pocket.

Will that day ever come? he asked himself. In his youth
he had assumed it would, and he had eagerly looked forward to it.

He raised his wine glass again and gazed at it absent-
mindedly. What a striking green color and what a fragrant
bouquet! But how could it ever compare with the beauty of
Hsiao Ch'ing's face and her intoxicating scent?

On a holiday in the autumn of 1965 Keng Erh and Hsiao
Ch'ing went to Fragrant Mountain to enjoy the maple leaves.
Since it was early in the season, the leaves at the base of the
mountain hadn't turned yet, and they took a walk up the
mountain to seek the brighter colors. Hsiao Ch'ing was
wearing a new lined jacket, and her shiny hair was neatly
braided and tied at the ends with red silk. As she walked
those two enchanting silk bands danced atop her shoulders.
Halfway up the mountain they came across a clump of maple
leaves that had turned red and stopped to admire them.
Hsiao Ch'ing picked a red leaf and handed it to him. Her
lips were brighter than the leaf, and Keng Erh could not keep
from taking her face in his hands and gently kissing her. She

did not try to resist him, though she blushed a deep crimson and kept her eyes lowered for a long time.

Ah, those days were beautiful beyond imagining. Keng Erh was walking on air. His heart was so full of love that he could not have expressed it if he had an eternity. It was like a stream that has been awakened from its winter sleep by a night of spring rain, suddenly so swollen it threatens to overflow its banks.

At forty, love had come to him late, but it had come nonetheless. He had known other women, but never had he been so swept off his feet. There had been very few Chinese girls around during his first few years in America, and since things in short supply are always cherished, those young women had been terribly disdainful of Chinese men and criticized their every flaw. And so Keng Erh decided to remove himself from the competition. As for American girls, they were ardent and unrestrained, and he found many who were responsive. He was tempted several times, but the thought that he would someday return to his own country made him unwilling to consider marriage. Thinking back to those austere times, those years of deprivation that finally led to a better life, Keng Erh realized that there hadn't been a single girl who could match the innocence, sincerity, and desirability of Hsiao Ch'ing.

Not only was he in love with her, but he was enchanted by her family as well. It was on the Sunday following their excursion to Fragrant Mountain that she first invited him to her home. Her parents were such kind old people that they immediately gained his complete respect and admiration. Old Mr. Hsüeh had spent half his life as a porter, but after

Liberation he was among the first batch of workers admitted
to the textile mill that had been constructed in Peking. He
had just retired that very year. His wife had given birth to
seven children, but only the last three had grown to adult-
hood: one son was serving in the army; their daughter was
honored every year as a model worker; and the youngest, also
a son, was about to graduate from middle school. And so the
old couple was perfectly content and full of gratitude to the
Communist Party. On the wall beside their brick bed hung
several newspaper photographs of Liu Shao-ch'i, Premier
Chou, and Chairman Mao.

On the day of the visit they had been preparing *chiao-tzu*,*
and although Keng Erh could not cook at all, during his years
in America he had learned how to make *chiao-tzu* skins.
So he rolled up his sleeves and set to work. He worked
quickly, and made each skin paper thin. The old couple was
astounded and showered him with praise. He had come with
misgivings, afraid that Hsiao Ch'ing's parents would be critical of his background, but they soon put him at ease and
treated him fondly, as they would their own son. Old Mr.
Hsüeh even asked him to stay to share his wine, and if it
hadn't been for Hsiao Ch'ing's presence, Keng Erh would
have let himself get roaring drunk that night. After dinner
Hsiao Ch'ing saw him out herself and walked hand in hand
with him past two bus stops before reluctantly letting him
get on a bus.

In his excitement he lay awake all that night, wondering

---

*Meat-filled dumplings that are steamed, cooked in boiling water, or
sometimes deep fried.

when to propose to her and trying to visualize how blissful their married life would be. He had only recently returned to China; filled with hope for the future, he was confident that he could find his niche in the new society. He had spent twenty-one years in school and then taught for ten years; this and the fact that his parents had also been teachers convinced him that he was a classic example of a petty bourgeois intellectual. A union with Hsiao Ch'ing, who came from a long line of workers, would mean not only a complete turnaround in his thoughts but also that his children would then inherit the noble blood of the working class. What could be more meaningful than that?

The next day Keng Erh skipped supper and rode his bicycle right from work to a department store where he spent the equivalent of three months' salary on an Omega watch as an engagement gift for Hsiao Ch'ing. He yearned to buy her all the beautiful things that were on display, but when he recalled her temperament, he just sighed. Although she had to contribute a large portion of her monthly salary of forty-two dollars to the support of her family, with high hopes and determination she had begun a savings plan so that in two years she would be able to buy a wristwatch made in Shanghai. She did not like Keng Erh to spend a lot of money on her, and sometimes insisted on treating him. Being used to the custom of giving flowers and gifts as a means of courting, Keng Erh was impressed by her independence and staunch self-respect, and he loved and admired her all the more for it. This girl of New China, ardent and yet solemn, gentle and yet strong, bewitched him no end.

It was in the midst of this, the greatest happiness he had

ever known, that the Great Cultural Revolution was ushered in. Never having been through a political campaign, Keng Erh welcomed it enthusiastically; once it has passed, he thought, he and Hsiao Ch'ing could be married. In the spring of 1966 she put in a verbal request at the textile mill and was told by her superiors that the matter could be taken care of after the campaign had run its course. But as the campaign spread and widened they had few opportunities to meet. With the coming of summer the Red Guards filled the streets, Hsiao Ch'ing's younger brother among them, and then Hsiao Ch'ing suggested that she and Keng Erh not be seen together because other people were "talking about them." This perplexed and pained him a great deal, for he never dreamed that Hsiao Ch'ing, who was so strong and independent, would be afraid of what other people were saying. But the most severe blow came when he returned from an assignment to find that she had sent back the wristwatch.

Suddenly a hush fell over the restaurant as everyone turned toward the head of the stairs. Keng Erh put down his empty glass and followed the others' glances. Two men dressed like cadre members were accompanying two other Chinese men in Western suits up to the next floor.

"Foreign visitors," the old man at his table said casually.

"Overseas Chinese," a young man at the next table spat out hatefully.

"I hear that the upper floor is reserved for foreigners," the old man said as he turned back to face Keng Erh.

"That's right," said Keng Erh. "Everything's the same, except that they eat in more comfortable surroundings."

"Is that so?" the old man replied, staring at Keng Erh.

Keng Erh said nothing as he busily added some noodles and cabbage to the pot. He did not want to disclose the fact that two weeks earlier he too had been up there, thanks to an old school friend from the University of Chicago, Professor Li. In the other man's wake he had climbed to the spacious and elegantly appointed upper level. The four men in their party had had a large room and several smiling waiters all to themselves.

"This is one of those unavoidable class problems during the transitional stage of a socialist society," the young man at the next table was saying sarcastically. "Once Communism becomes a reality the upper floor will be abolished and everyone will stand in line for tickets and eat with the crowd downstairs."

"Here's hoping that Communism will be here soon!" His associate—also a young man—raised his beer glass.

Keng Erh exchanged glances with the old man, then lowered his head and took a bite of his wheat cake.

The thought of his schoolmate filled him with mixed emotions. In America their political views had been worlds apart, and their arguments had often ended in angry partings. But this time when they met they had been very cordial to one another. When Professor Li discovered that Keng Erh was still a bachelor, he slapped him on the back and asked in disbelief, "What? Still unattached after all these years?" Keng Erh just smiled and said nothing.

"You know, Lao Keng, you're not getting any younger. You shouldn't be too particular," said his old friend.

Keng Erh could only smile wryly and change the subject.

He didn't want to tell his friend that the status of the intellectuals had plummeted since the Cultural Revolution, especially since the fall of 1968, when Chairman Mao directed that all intellectuals be reeducated by the workers, peasants, and soldiers. The intellectuals had to bow their heads and submit meekly to reeducation, and they all became outcasts in the new society. So how could he be particular in choosing a mate? It was commendable that his old schoolmate, who had long since become an American citizen, had come back to China to celebrate China's National Day, and Keng Erh did not want to dampen his enthusiasm. Besides, since he now took pride in his leftist leanings, he was both unable and unwilling to accept certain facts.

"Reeducation"—as he dwelled on the word, a coldness gripped him. For the past couple of years it was seldom used, but every time he heard it his heart sank, just as it did when he first heard that Hsiao Ch'ing had become a member of the Workers' Corps for the Propagation of the Thought of Mao Tse-tung (nicknamed Workers' Publicity Corps). One day toward the end of 1968 Keng Erh rode his bicycle to a spot beyond Ch'ao Yang Gate—even though his love had miscarried because of the Cultural Revolution, he often came there—and ran into Hsiao Ch'ing's younger brother. At one time he had been a proud and overbearing Red Guard leader, but his prestige had evidently waned considerably. Quite unexpectedly it was he who called out to Keng Erh. Keng Erh first inquired about the boy's parents, and then inevitably about Hsiao Ch'ing.

"My sister is a member of the Workers' Publicity Corps!" the boy stated proudly. "She no longer lives at home. Her section has been assigned to the Peking Technology University and she's the assistant section leader."

Keng Erh regretted that he believed in no religion, for he wished he could pray to someone that Hsiao Ch'ing not be assigned to the Academy of Sciences. From that time on, whenever he came across a haughty member of the Workers' Publicity Corps in the Academy, he would immediately think of Hsiao Ch'ing, and his heart would throb.

There is nothing more painful than to be reminded of one's secret sorrow. Unhappily for Keng Erh, such reminders came often. The week before was a case in point: After a joyful excursion to the Motherland's scenic highlights, Professor Li invited Keng Erh to eat at the hotel restaurant. Since it was Professor Li's last night in Peking, the two men talked far into the night, reminiscing about old times, and the subject of Keng Erh's marriage was raised again.

"Lao Keng, you really ought to take my advice," Professor Li said hesitatingly, hoping to avoid any misunderstanding. "A woman doesn't have to be a college graduate to be a good wife. As I understand it, the standard of education is quite high throughout the country. The workers here in Peking are nice. Oh, yes, the day before yesterday I toured the Third Textile Mill and I saw quite a few pretty young girls there."

Perhaps it was because he had drunk too much *maotai** wine, or perhaps he wanted to see if he could face up to his unhappy love affair, but whatever the reason, Keng Erh con-

---

*A strong wine, almost a liqueur.

fided in his friend. His old schoolmate listened to the whole story and was both surprised and sympathetic.

"Is she married now?"

Keng Erh shook his head. "I don't know." Although he had never made any inquiries, he was pretty sure that she was not married. Twice in the past two years he had caught a glimpse of her, and on both occasions she had been alone.

"I think you should go to see her right away," Professor Li said earnestly. "If she isn't married yet, there's still plenty of hope. Isn't there supposed to be a positive attitude toward the intellectuals these days? Who ever heard of a person being ineligible for marriage just because he is a high-level intellectual? Since the working class is supposed to assume leadership in everything, all the more reason for them to marry intellectuals. That way they can facilitate their re-education!"

His friend clapped his hands and roared with laughter at his own witticism. Keng Erh laughed along with him, but there was no laughter in his heart. He was thinking of that day in 1971 when he had seen her across Tienanmen Square —walking all alone across the Bridge of Golden Waters, her head held high, her hair still in braids, but her face serious and her eyes fixed straight ahead. In his excitement, he had barely been able to hold his bicycle steady, and it had taken all his will power to keep from calling out to her. Suddenly drained of his strength, he had pedalled weakly across the square. How he had longed to hold her hands and speak intimately to her, to gaze at length into her eyes, which shone like two meteors on a wintry night. But his courage had left him.

"I understand that this earth-shaking Cultural Revolution has changed a great many people, and that everything has taken on a new look," Professor Li said. "It seems you've changed a great deal yourself."

Keng Erh nodded in agreement.

"For better or worse?"

"That depends on your definition of what is good and what is bad," Keng Erh answered with a smile.

"You're always so mysterious with me. But let's get back to the matter at hand. I'll be seeing a certain high official tomorrow; would you like me to discuss your problem with him?"

"No, no!" Keng Erh shouted.

My God! His heart cried out against sending someone to Hsiao Ch'ing, who "held the reins of leadership," recommending that in response to the policy toward intellectuals, she should marry so-and-so.

Shaking his head violently, he said resolutely, "I've gotten used to living alone and I no longer think about getting married."

"Then you must have devoted all your energy to your work. You must have published quite a few papers over the past few years."

Keng Erh smiled as he shook his head again. "We place importance only on practical work at the Academy, not on publishing; our emphasis is on cooperative ventures, not on individual projects."

How could he tell his friend that he had in fact changed his field, that the program at the institute was constantly shifting to suit the needs of the revolution? In the final analysis, I am a Chinese, he told himself: how I feel is my own business, but defending the national image is a moral obligation. This most likely is the dialectical application of Mao's "one divides into two" theory.

It was getting late, and Keng Erh got up to leave, but his old schoolmate was loath to say goodbye and walked him to the door of the hotel, switching to English as he said to him, "Lao Keng, is there anything you would like me to do for you?"

After a moment's thought, Keng Erh smiled and answered, "Yes, there is. Come back often, so I can go along with you to restaurants reserved for foreign visitors. That would give me more pleasure than anything else."

More pleasure than anything else!

"Hm?" The old man across the table was staring at him. "What were you saying?"

Keng Erh realized that he had forgotten himself again, but he was beginning to feel the effects of the wine, so he answered without embarrassment, "I was saying that eating mutton fire pot gives me more pleasure than anything else."

"I agree, I agree completely," the old man said, nodding vigorously.

The two of them picked up pieces of mutton with their chopsticks and ate with gusto.

II

A few days before the Lunar New Year's holidays some of Keng Erh's unmarried colleagues began leaving Peking to join their families, and those who remained did not feel much like working. On the final day of the old year they managed to drag through the morning, and not long after lunch they too left. Alone in the deserted institute, Keng Erh had no desire to stick around, so he left before three o'clock and went home to his dormitory.

The Lunar New Year* is still the most important Chinese festival, with a tradition of thousands of years. Even the preparation of food is much more elaborate than that of the National Day celebrations. Keng Erh could hear the other people in the dormitory chopping and mincing meat to make the filling for *chiao-tzu*; in fact the same sound had awakened him early that morning.

He removed his hat and gloves and took his customary turn through the bedroom and the living room. His apartment was even quieter and more deserted than the institute. Ten years earlier, when he moved into the two-room apartment, he found it too small and crowded, but the longer he lived there, the bigger and the emptier it seemed. He often secretly congratulated himself, for in Peking it was rare indeed for a single person to have a two-room place with room to walk around in.

He felt tired, so he headed for the kitchen to make a cup of coffee to drive out the cold and pick him up a bit. Over the last couple of years he had stopped drinking coffee in the afternoon, for fear that it would keep him awake at night, but this was New Year's eve and he seized upon the excuse.

Keng Erh had given Wang Ta-sao,† his housekeeper, a

---

*The Lunar New Year usually occurs in the month of February.
†Literally "elder sister-in-law," Ta-sao is used here as a courtesy title.

week off over the holidays. He didn't feel any need to straighten up the place—it would be strange indeed if anyone came to see him—and so his bed was in disarray, looking as though he had just gotten out of it. He could not abide the job of washing his own clothes, so he simply did not change his shirt; if he had, there would be a pile of dirty clothes awaiting Wang Ta-sao's return. That could be interpreted as exploiting her labor, despite the fact that as she was leaving she repeatedly told him—almost begged him—to leave his clothes for her to wash when she returned.

"I'm a bachelor, through and through," he thought aloud as he entered the kitchen.

There was a mountain of dirty dishes in the sink, and he would have to wash a cup before he could have some coffee. He dug out the tea kettle, washed it, filled it with water, and placed it on the stove. Then he found a match and lit the stove. He turned around and opened the refrigerator, from which he removed a can of Shanghai coffee. The refrigerator, a Westinghouse, was in operation only for two months during the summer; the rest of the year it was not plugged in, and merely served as a cupboard. For one thing, electricity was too costly (it wouldn't have bothered him to hand over an extra ten dollars a month, but he was concerned that people might talk); for another, he normally ate in the cafeteria.

The great hulking object left very little space in the tiny kitchen even to turn around. Keng Erh reflected that it might have been better in the long run if the Red Guards had taken the thing along with them while they were on their property confiscation binge!

The pity of it was that they had gone about their confiscation in such a refined fashion. Perhaps that particular group of Red Guards had been so courteous to him because it was made up of children of his colleagues at the Academy. All they had done was to open the refrigerator door out of curiosity, turn a few somersaults on his box-spring bed, and dig out some of the Western suits from his trunk. After poking a few jokes at his clothes, they had left. The destruction of his twenty-year collection of newspaper clippings regarding space exploration had pained him at the time, but then saving those really didn't serve any purpose, so why not just commit them to the flames? After all, the Chinese certainly were in no hurry to travel to the moon. Yet despite the kid-glove treatment, two years after the incident the State Council sent him a letter of apology, which had been formalized with a large red official seal. If anything, that proved an embarrassment to him, for compared to the treatment received by a number of other families, his losses could hardly be considered significant. Some time later a colleague informed him that Premier Chou had heard reports about the confiscation of property belonging to returned scholars from Europe and America who were working at the Academy, and had ordered that returned technicians and scientists be given favored treatment.

Long Live Premier Chou! Keng Erh silently wished him all the best.

The water was boiling. Keng Erh dug around for a moment and located a spoon. He put two scoops of coffee in the pot, replaced the lid, and turned the fire low.

For Premier Chou he held the greatest respect and admiration. In 1973, just as the Anti-Lin Piao, Anti-Confucius campaign was getting under way, many people were saying privately that although the president of the Academy of Sciences, Kuo Mo-jo, was under attack, the point of the spear was actually aimed at the Premier. Keng Erh was concerned for Chou En-lai, particularly during the first half of 1974, when for several months the Premier made no public appearances. Underground reports were rampant, all of which depressed and disconcerted Keng Erh. He was finally able to relax a bit when he read in the newspaper that the Premier was laid up in the hospital.

Keng Erh closed his eyes and breathed deeply, letting the aroma of coffee refresh him. He rinsed the tea cup he had used in the morning, and reminded himself that he would have to wash all those dishes before Wang Ta-sao returned. He found the filter he had bought at the herb medicine shop and poured his coffee through it.

He very carefully carried the cup into the next room, sat down at his desk, and slowly sipped his coffee. His combination living room and study contained only a desk, two chairs, a wastebasket, and a full bookcase. On his desk stood three Christmas cards from America, which he now read once more. He had received them a long time ago, and the senders had all wanted to know what his "present situation" was, but he had never answered any of them. The truth was that he didn't know what to say; present or past situation, it made no difference since there was really nothing worth telling. It dawned on him that these cards had already fulfilled their mission, so what was the use of keeping them around? He gathered them up and threw them in the wastebasket.

Without doubt, America wasted more paper than any

other country on earth. Why, in greeting cards alone, there was a congratulatory variety for every imaginable occasion, and condolence cards for the passing of a loved one; and people often received get-well cards for minor ailments. Dispensing with all this ceremony in China resulted in savings in time and energy; although . . . although what? Keng Erh shook his head without quite knowing why, then took a long drink of coffee.

He saw by the clock on his desk that it was three-thirty. He checked his wristwatch—three-thirty on the nose. At six o'clock he had to be at the home of his colleague Hsiao Chang. During the past couple of years he had rarely visited Hsiao Chang, so the invitation, extended the week before, for New Year's dinner had come as a surprise. Perhaps they sympathize with me because I'm alone, and they are afraid that my New Year's will be dreary, he thought. His first reaction was to refuse and thereby save himself from being reminded of a more recent sorrow. But Hsiao Chang dropped by again only the day before to urge him to come over. The prospect of eating New Year's dinner in the cafeteria was very unpleasant (the head cook was on vacation and the apprentice was taking his place in the kitchen; add to that the depressing atmosphere of the nearly deserted cafeteria), so he cheerfully accepted the invitation.

Hsiao Chang was thirty-five or thirty-six years old, but everyone called him "Hsiao" because there was another fellow named Chang at the Academy, whom they called Lao Chang or "Old" Chang; in order to avoid confusion, he was stuck with the appellation "Little." He did research in the physics institute, having been a very bright graduate of the

Shanghai Communications College. Although his origins were far from ideal, he was content with what he was and with his lot, so that during the Cultural Revolution he didn't suffer too much. Keng Erh had met him at an academic conference, following which Hsiao Chang came to ask him about some geophysical data, and from then on they got to know each other well. Possibly it was because they worked in different institutions, and because Hsiao Chang did not live in the dormitory of the Academy—he and his wife lived in the dormitory of her unit—that he was so eager to associate with Keng Erh. In the past he had often invited Keng Erh over to relax and enjoy himself, though in the course of a year it was unusual if he came over to Keng Erh's dormitory at all.

No matter what, I really should call on them, Keng Erh thought as he sipped his coffee. Certainly they have been genuinely concerned about me, and even though Hsiao Kin and I didn't get married, Hsiao Chang and his wife have done everything they could.

In the spring of 1971, Mrs. Chang's cousin Hsiao Kin had come to Peking on a holiday. Since she was staying with the Changs, Hsiao Chang made a point of introducing her to Keng Erh, but first he told Keng Erh all about her. Hsiao Kin was thirty, fair-skinned, with rather small eyes. She had recently been widowed, but had no children. "She's a graduate of a normal school, which is roughly the same as being a university student, even though she doesn't really meet the standards you've set." Hsiao Chang couldn't keep from smiling as he said this.

Ai! Not only had Keng Erh blushed then, but he grew

uneasy thinking about the conversation even now. It harked back to a tremendous blunder he had committed almost the moment he had set foot in the country, and for which he knew he would be a laughingstock for the rest of his life. Shortly after he had taken up his post, one of the unit leaders sought him out for a chat and asked if there was anything he particularly desired. Without thinking, Keng Erh blurted out that he hoped to get married at an early date, to which the leader nodded repeatedly without saying a word. Before long a colleague who was passing the time of day with him asked what qualities he envisioned for his ideal wife. Without a moment's hesitation he answered that she should be a college graduate with large eyes and fair skin, and shouldn't be over thirty. How could he have known that this would become common knowledge, and that everyone would snicker and shake their heads, saying that his conditions were far too rigid? When he realized that everyone was talking about him, Keng Erh's embarrassment knew no bounds.

And yet his first meeting with Hsiao Kin proved very satisfying. She was born and raised in Kweilin, and that "land of unsurpassed scenic beauty" seemed to have endowed her with a certain appeal. She was small in stature, had fair skin and an oval face, and her hair was cut in what was commonly called the overseas Chinese fashion. Although her eyes were on the small side, she was well groomed, and Keng Erh simply could not tell that she was thirty and had already been married.

Hsiao Kin, too, seemed pleased by what she saw, and when Mrs. Chang proposed that Keng Erh take her to the Summer Palace on Worker's Day, she readily agreed and even suggested a place to meet. As expected, their outing turned out very well, and from then on, Keng Erh had a standing date to take her out every Sunday.

He tried very hard to forget Hsiao Ch'ing, but he soon realized that his efforts were in vain, and he only could hope that the shadow of his past would in no way affect his marriage.

The two women were so different that he sometimes found himself subjecting them to comparison. When Hsiao Ch'ing had fallen in love she was still very young, and the future held many dreams for her. Hsiao Kin, on the other hand, was a mature woman who harbored no illusions. She was primarily concerned with what she could get out of life. She was realistic and practical, and obviously an ideal housewife. She asked the same question about everything: "Is it worth it?" There were times when Keng Erh dared not imagine the measure of his own worth in her eyes. From their very first meeting he was aware of how warm and considerate she was toward him. She loved to talk, but on those occasions when Keng Erh was in a pensive mood, she managed to keep her tongue in check and sit quietly.

Hsiao Kin was a great admirer of Western things, and liked to be taken to Western-style restaurants. And even though to Keng Erh the steak might be so well done it was like chewing wax, she would eat it with gusto. And what about the mutton fire pot, of which he never grew tired? Once seemed to be enough for her. Keng Erh invited her to his dormitory during the mid-autumn festival for a cup of coffee (it was also his intention to let everyone see that he had found someone). She went over the two rooms very carefully, looking at everything and praising his mahogany box-spring bed, his wardrobe, and his refrigerator. She touched them all lovingly and lingered over them all.

"What a beautiful bed! Such fine wood! You really should have brought more furniture with you when you came back."

But Keng Erh was embarrassed; he blushed and was at a loss for words. Hsiao Kin couldn't have known how much he regretted having shipped this furniture over when he returned to China. For many years it was an emotional burden to him. Hsiao Ch'ing had also been aware that he owned a refrigerator, but she had never even wanted to see it. What different women they were!

Keng Erh had trouble reconciling the fact that he was Hsiao Kin's senior by sixteen years, and for that reason he hesitated to make his feelings known. But Hsiao Kin seemed to read his mind and gave him a lot of encouragement. She often hinted, and sometimes commented openly, that he was still robust, that he didn't show his age, and that he walked briskly, like a young man.

Keng Erh was also aided by the census check. In 1971, as the National Day drew near, out-of-town residents were not being allowed to remain in Peking. Neighborhood committees had been mobilized to urge visitors who had no official business to leave as soon as possible. Since Hsiao Kin had been in Peking for more than four months, the local neighborhood committee had already been to see her three times and ordered her to return to Kweilin before the National Day. The day after Hsiao Chang passed this information on, Keng Erh asked Hsiao Kin to join him for dinner, and he proposed to her in the restaurant. She accepted happily and readily, without the slightest trace of feminine shyness. On the contrary, she urged Keng Erh to turn in the marriage request soon, and then she wrote down the date of her birth, her family background, her occupation, and her work history. "I'll be in Kweilin waiting for news from you," she said warmly, her small eyes looking at him ardently, her soft white hand holding his. Keng Erh squeezed her small hand, and in the midst of the noisy crowd of people, they sat in silence, smiling at each other.

Keng Erh arranged for Hsiao Kin's train ticket and bought her many gifts. Two days before October First, he went with Hsiao Chang to see her off on the southbound train. Immediately after the National Day Keng Erh submitted his marriage request. When his colleagues at the institute found out that he was going to marry a pretty little widow, they all congratulated him heartily, and some of the women even offered to help with the wedding. Keng Erh was so happy he was even singing a few snatches from a revolutionary opera.

After submitting his request he lived in a state of happy anticipation. Two weeks went by, and his department head informed him that his superiors were giving the request careful consideration, and he would be informed the moment the decision was made. Keng Erh was puzzled. Giving it careful consideration? After all, this is me, Keng Erh, who's getting married, he thought. Why does someone else need to give the matter consideration? Experience told him that accepting everything as arranged was the best stratagem, so he said nothing. But as 1971 came to a close and no news was forthcoming, he grew anxious. Once he even brazenly asked for some news, and his department head told him that the institute authorities were just then checking into Comrade Kin's family background and that he should be patient. Anger filled his heart, but he remained silent. Hsiao Kin continued to write fervent letters, but he had no good news to report to her.

Before long Keng Erh was sent to a farm in Kiangsi for six months' labor reform, and the matter was shelved for the time being. Following that, he was given an out-of-town assignment that lasted several months, and by the time he returned it was already the fall of 1972. He had long since lost the courage to ask for news. One political campaign followed another, all of them major events involving the national leadership and the integrity of the nation, so of what importance was one individual's marriage?

One day during a break in the political discussion period, the head of Keng Erh's department asked him if he still had any contact with Hsiao Kin. The question put him on guard, and he had a feeling of impending disappointment. "I haven't heard from her for a long time. I'm not even sure where she is now," he answered.

His reply seemed to please the department head, who seemed to know what was on Keng Erh's mind. "It's for the best if you sever your relationship with her. You see, her background is no good. Her father was a landlord and her husband's status was no better, for his father was one of the Kwangsi Clique warlords. Toward the end of the Cultural Revolution her husband was investigated in conjunction with the Cleansing of the Class Ranks, but before the results of the investigation were known, he 'terminated his ties with the Party and the people'—committed suicide—and so his political status remains unclear. As for her, she was originally a middle-school teacher. In 1970 she was directed to go into the countryside and work on a farm, but she made excuses that her parents' health was poor, so she remained in Kweilin. Later on she went off somewhere for a long period of time. For those of us who work in a highly sensitive spot such as the Academy of Sciences, a wife with this sort of background is certainly not ideal. Our superiors are very concerned about your marital situation, and it's on the minds of your colleagues as well . . ."

The department head had quite a bit more to say, but Keng Erh heard none of it. He could only congratulate himself that he was old enough to keep his emotions under control. Rather than explode in rage, he actually nodded his head very politely in agreement. But deep down in his heart he cried in despair, Why, why did I have to work in the Academy of Sciences?

At first he felt sorry only for himself, but late at night when everything was quiet and he sat down to write a letter to Hsiao Kin, he saw how unjustly she was being treated. Of what crime was she guilty? She was being forced to suffer for the sins of her parents and of her deceased husband. Reportedly she had not responded to Chairman Mao's call, and she stood accused of vanity and cherishing city life. But Keng Erh, who had spent time in the countryside as duty demanded, did not have the heart to criticize her for these failings. It was clear, of course, that there was no hope for their union. Keng Erh hadn't written to her for a long time, but he was afraid that Hsiao Kin would continue to wait in vain and waste her youth. He was also unwilling to divulge the true situation. In the end he told her somewhat ambiguously that his superiors felt that their ages were too disparate and that even he felt strongly that it was an unwise match. He asked for her forgiveness and wished her every happiness.

After mailing the letter he felt that he had let Hsiao Kin down, but he also felt that he had been seriously wronged, and he yearned to find a place where he could give vent to his rage. Unhappily, no such place existed. He wasn't willing to reveal his disappointment to his superiors and his colleagues for fear that they would laugh at him for being discouraged just because he couldn't find a wife. Concealing his emotions provided to be the most difficult thing of all.

He soon discovered that he tired very easily and that although he longed for rest, he suffered from insomnia. When he was at work his mind often wandered, and even his memory, of which he had always been so proud, began to fail him. He knew without consulting a physician that he was suffering from a typical case of neurotic depression, for which there was no medication.

Shortly afterward Lin Piao's attempted coup and death were reported. The official proclamations and the rumors about this perplexing incident drove Keng Erh to distraction. He was unclear as to just who was being victimized— he himself, Lin Piao, or possibly Chairman Mao. He felt that he had been deprived of his last remaining shred of faith, and he was as helpless as a blind man who has lost his cane. Then he caught a cold, and had to stay in bed. As he had not been ill for many years, his superiors and colleagues were greatly concerned and showered him with sympathy. He was glad to take a few days of sick leave, even though he knew that there was really nothing wrong with him. He simply needed to rest, to sleep, to lie in bed and do nothing but stare at the ceiling.

He had already recovered and was back on the job when he received Hsiao Kin's reply. Warm and considerate as ever, she alluded to the past with fondness and tried to gloss over her disappointment. She treasured their friendship, she said at the end of her letter, and hoped that they would continue to correspond. When it was clear that she did not reproach him in the least, Keng Erh felt somewhat better. Someone as alert as Hsiao Kin would have seen the truth—perhaps Hsiao Chang had told her, for he sensed things earlier and more acutely than most people, and he had already found out the actual circumstances of the matter, even though he never mentioned it to Keng Erh. Keng Erh did not believe that Hsiao Chang would blame him, and their meetings were always friendly; still, they no longer got together very often.

Keng Erh did a quick calculation and realized that he hadn't been in the Chang home for precisely two years. "Ling-ling and T'ing-t'ing are always asking about you," Hsiao Chang had said to him the previous day. Keng Erh and the two little girls had been great friends.

It suddenly occurred to Keng Erh that he had to have New Year's presents for the children and that it was now four o'clock. He had long since finished his coffee, so he put the cup back in the kitchen sink. He gave the clothes he was wearing the once-over. His pants were soiled but instead of changing them he decided to put on a pair of dacron over-trousers. He made sure that his wallet was in the pocket of his padded cotton jacket; put on a cap, a scarf, and gloves; and left. Hsiao Chang lived outside West Gate, but first Keng Erh had to ride into the city to buy what he needed.

Except for the big red couplets recently pasted on either side of the entrance to the department store, all the New Year's greetings had revolutionary themes. There was a festive air among the people on the streets, even though there were no special holiday decorations in sight, and the department store was still crowded with customers. Keng Erh was surprised to see so many people in the same predicament as he, still buying presents on the last night of the year.

He went first to the confection counter, where he eyed the tins of cookies in the showcase as he stood in line.

"What do you want?" asked a clerk whose eyelids were so droopy he seemed about to fall asleep.

"I'd like a tin of T'ai-k'ang Cookies," he said, pointing to the largest and most attractive tin.

"They're not for sale!" the clerk said impatiently, raising his eyebrows and sneering at him.

"Well . . ." Keng Erh wasn't sure what he should do now. "Well, what kinds are for sale?"

"Do you want expensive ones?" The clerk's eyes were now wide open as he sized up his customer.

"Yes. Yes, I do."

The clerk took out a tin of T'ien-shan Cookies. "This is eight-fifty."

"Are they rationed?" asked a customer with an out-of-town accent who was standing behind Keng Erh. He closed in and enviously touched the tin.

"Of course not. Ration coupons aren't required for expensive items," another customer interjected, with a sarcastic ring. "Eight-fifty! There couldn't be more than two catties in the tin. Cookies in bulk sell for less than two dollars a catty!"

Just as Keng Erh was about to say something, a hand reached in alongside him.

"Let me have a tin too!"

Everyone turned to look. It was a soldier, holding a ten dollar bill in his other hand.

"All right, all right!" the clerk answered, momentarily revitalized.

"I want a box of chocolates, too," Keng Erh quickly added. "That is, if you have them in metal tins."

"None in metal tins. How about those wrapped in tinfoil? They're from Shanghai and make excellent gifts."

"All right, they're fine. Give me twenty."

"Twenty!" The clerk's eyes were really wide open now. "These are all we have left." He placed the entire supply on the counter.

"All right, that'll do," said Keng Erh, taking his money out of his pocket. "Could I trouble you to wrap it all up together?"

Keng Erh quickly picked up his parcel and virtually flew from the confection counter and the stares of everyone present. Fortunately there weren't many people at the salted meats counter. He purchased several catties of Hunan salted meat and Cantonese-style sausage. Then he bought some apples at a fruit stand. By now his hands were full and it was getting late, so he left the store. He attached one package to the handlebars and carefully tied the rest to the book rack on the back of his bicycle. Then he slowly rode west.

The sky turned dark and cold before six o'clock. The city itself was bustling, but after Keng Erh left the West Gate district the streets were much quieter. The vehicles on the road seemed to be moving a little faster. The bicyclists rode with their noses and mouths covered by white masks, as they leaned over their handlebars and pedalled energetically in anticipation of their year-end family dinners. Keng Erh let quite a few of them pass him, feeling that he was probably the only one who wasn't in any particular hurry.

The large dormitory complex where the Changs lived looked a little unfamiliar to him, since he hadn't been there for two years, but he quickly found their place and parked his bicycle by the door.

Hsiao Chang stuck his head out. "Lao Keng, you made it!" He hurried out the door.

"Say there, Hsiao Chang! Am I late?"

"No, we're just getting ready to eat!" Hsiao Chang came out to help Keng Erh with his bundles. "It was enough just for you to come. You didn't have to bring all these packages too!"

"It's New Year's—it's for the children. How are they?"

No sooner had he asked the question than they appeared in the doorway, both dressed in fancy new sweaters. The older one remained standing by the door, but the younger one ran over to Keng Erh and tugged on his coat. She looked up at him, and said, "Uncle Keng, you haven't been to see us for a long time."

"Ah, Ling-ling, look how tall you've grown!" Keng Erh bent over and cheerfully stroked her little braid. "Are you in school now?"

"Not yet," her father answered for her. "She was born on September first, and since there were too few openings this year, she didn't qualify. She'll have to wait till next fall. By then she'll be seven years old, so there shouldn't be any problem."

"That's a shame, but then starting school a year late doesn't make that much difference."

"That's right," Hsiao Chang agreed. "Later when she goes out to the farm, if she's a little older it will be to her advantage, since she'll be able to wield the hoe better."

"Uncle Keng," the older daughter called out to their guest. She was demure and a little self-conscious.

"Ah, T'ing-t'ing, I almost didn't recognize you. You're getting prettier all the time. What grade are you in now?"

"Fourth," she answered shyly, as she stood aside to let everyone else pass.

As he stepped inside Keng Erh could smell the sweet-and-sour pork and could hear the food sizzling in the pan.

Hsiao Chang's one-and-a-half room apartment—one room was so small that Chang jokingly referred to it as half a room—was filled to capacity with furniture, quite the opposite of Keng Erh's. The larger room measured only ten by ten but the Changs had squeezed in a bed, a desk that also served as a dinner table, a bookcase, and a sewing machine. The space beneath the bed was crammed full, and things were even hanging from the ceiling. The smaller room held only a bed.

"Please have a seat," said Hsiao Chang, as he placed the parcels on the bed. Keng Erh put the package of salted meats in the only unoccupied space, on top of the sewing machine. Hsiao Chang sat down alongside the table, which had been placed at the head of the bed, thereby eliminating the need for a chair. The two girls immediately nestled up to him, one on either side. The dinner table had been set and two dishes had already been placed in the center: a steaming bowl of stewed meat and one of mixed meat and vegetables.

"How has your wife been lately?"

"Fine, just fine; about the same as the rest of us, spending her time poring over documents, trying to understand every word." As he was speaking, Mrs. Chang walked in carrying a plate of food, a broad grin on her face.

"Mr. Keng, how are you?"

"Fine, thank you, just fine."

He rose to his feet, but before he could finish what he was saying, another woman carrying a plate of food came into the room. It was Hsiao Kin. Keng Erh was so surprised he was at a loss for words and just stood there dumbly.

"How are you, Lao Keng?" The smile on her face could not entirely hide her nervousness.

"When . . . did you arrive in Peking?" It took him some time before he was able to pick up the conversation.

"Just two days ago," Mrs. Chang answered for her cousin.

"Come on, sit down," said Hsiao Chang, ceremoniously.

Mrs. Chang put the two plates on the table and made Hsiao Kin sit down.

"Kin Chieh,* you don't have to come out into the kitchen; I'll bring the soup when it's ready. Go ahead, and see that everyone is served."

Mrs. Chang wiped her hands on her apron and went back to the kitchen.

At first glance, Hsiao Kin seemed unchanged. Her clothing was a bit more colorful and better made, her short hair was very neat, and when she smiled her dimples were as captivating as ever. She was just as unaffected, but her eyes didn't seem as clear and spirited as they had in the past. Then Keng Erh noticed wrinkles at the corners of her eyes. We're all getting older! He sighed inwardly.

"You seem slimmer," he said.

"Really?" There was a hint of sadness in her voice. At the same time she unconsciously tidied up her already smooth short hair. T'ing-t'ing brought out a pot of rice, and Hsiao Kin began to fill everyone's bowl. Hsiao Chang went to the bookcase for a bottle of cherry wine.

"Well, what have we here! Where did you get that?" Keng Erh asked enviously. He didn't care much for sweet wines, but things always seem more precious when they are scarce, and wine like that could not be bought on the open market.

"Ha! It wasn't easy!" Hsiao Chang said proudly as he searched for a bottle opener. "The fellow in our institute from England, Lao Lo—do you know who I mean? Well,

---

*Literally "Elder Sister Kin."

around the first of the year an old schoolmate of his from
England came to Peking to visit some relatives, and he
stopped off to see him while he was in the vicinity. On a
sudden inspiration, I asked Lo to see if his guest could buy a
few things for me at the Friendship Store, and that's how I
managed to get my hands on this bottle of wine and the
Shanghai sweaters the girls are wearing. Those sweaters cost
the same as the ones on the market, but they're of much
better quality!"

A few moments later Mrs. Chang carried in a potful of
soup cooked with a whole chicken. The table wasn't big
enough to begin with, and since the two children liked the
idea of eating by themselves, Chang finally had them take
their food into the adjoining room. When Mrs. Chang had
removed her apron and was seated at the table opposite
Hsiao Kin, Chang raised his wine glass and toasted Keng Erh.
"Here we go, bottoms up! Good luck to everyone!"

"Here's hoping that everything goes well for everyone this
New Year's holiday!" Hsiao Kin added.

Neither of the women was accustomed to drinking wine;
Mrs. Chang managed to drink half a glass, while Hsiao Kin
took only one sip and set her glass down as though she had
something on her mind. Keng Erh couldn't tell what she
was thinking and was embarrassed to ask what had brought
her to Peking. He had received a letter from her only the
month before, and there was no mention of any plans for a
visit. Even more important to him was how long she was
planning to stay this time, but he had no opportunity to
ask. The talk around the table was mainly of national affairs,
such as Chou En-lai's continued role as helmsman, and the

formal appearance on the scene of Teng Hsiao-p'ing.

"With older men in charge, we can all take it a little easier," Hsiao Chang commented with feeling. "There have just been too many ups and downs these past few years, and every time the leftists are in power we are all in for a rough time."

"You'd better keep that sort of rightist talk in the home, or you'll wind up wearing a label!" Mrs. Chang warned her husband. She was a very affable woman, short and stout, her face never without a smile.

"Hai! Don't you worry. At the institute I've always tested the winds and I'm right there with every change of course," Hsiao Chang said. "When they were integrating the archaeological excavation of the Chou dynasty tombs with the Anti-Lin Piao, Anti-Confucius campaign, the statement I wrote was in demand even by the Propaganda Section."

"Hsiao Chang really does have a knack for writing," praised Keng Erh. Whenever he had to write political criticism he could never think of what to say. He couldn't help admiring Chang's talent.

"You're being too polite," Hsiao Chang protested humbly. "I'm not in the same league with the young fellows in the archaeological institute. In all honesty, they've dug up quite a few objects these past few years, and that's proved very stimulating to them. The pity is that they lag behind in arranging, laboratory analysis, and preservation techniques, so that some of the objects have changed color after being unearthed, and may have even fallen apart."

Mrs. Chang suddenly laughed. "My, I don't know how you integrated the Anti-Lin Piao, Anti-Confucius campaigns, but it was quite something at our unit. The last time we had a big criticism meeting, one of the workers got up to speak. He began by reading a prepared text, but the more aroused he grew, the more impromptu his talk became. He said that Lin the Bald One had predicted that New China was going to revert back to Confucian times, where the majority of people would be slaves and the minority would act as the nobility. 'Comrades, how can we accept this kind of reactionary talk?' Those of us at the foot of the podium naturally began shouting our unqualified rejection of such a policy. But then we glanced at one another, wondering when and where Lin Piao could have uttered such absurdities as those!"

"It's the same everywhere, people aping others," Keng Erh commented with a smile.

"You'll be all right if you just get on the bandwagon quickly," said Hsiao Chang as he refilled Keng Erh's glass. "Come on, Lao Keng, this is what really counts: 'Here is wine, let us sing/For man's life is short.' "*

And so they ate and chatted, holding nothing back, passing the time pleasantly. Keng Erh discovered that Hsiao Kin wasn't as lively and talkative as before; she was more demure and dignified, and lovelier than ever. He hoped that her stay in Peking, like her last visit, could be an extended one, and he longed to spend that time with her. Not having seen her for more than a year, and now finding himself sitting beside her, he felt not only excitement but comfort as well; it was as though the accumulated fatigue had been erased in a

---

*The first two lines (with one word changed) of a poem by Ts'ao Ts'ao (Emperor Wu of the Wei dynasty).

moment. As he gazed at her pink cheeks and her small hand holding the chopsticks, his heart started pounding faster and faster. A great many visions crowded into his mind, particularly of two days he and Hsiao Kin had spent together in Kweilin.

As though on cue, Mrs. Chang started to talk about Kweilin, where she had spent her youth. She still had cherished memories of that beautiful region.

"Do you still go to Great Dipper Crag or to the place they just discovered, Reed Flute Crag?" she asked her cousin. But before Hsiao Kin had a chance to answer, Mrs. Chang put down her chopsticks and continued enviously, "I wonder when I'll be able to go to Kweilin again. How lucky you are not to have to worry about being sent down to the countryside anymore. As a matter of fact, as I see it, you don't ever have to worry about work assignments at all."

Hsiao Kin quickly cut her short, "Why not find an excuse this summer to take a few days off?" Then she turned to Keng Erh and said with a smile, "Kweilin is even lovelier than ever. If you're sent to Kwangsi on assignment again, make sure you come to Kweilin for another visit."

"How could it not be lovely!" Hsiao Chang interjected. "It's one of the places that's on every foreign tourist's itinerary."

At the word "tourist," Hsiao Kin asked Keng Erh, "Do you still remember Han Suyin? I read that she recently gave a speech at Hong Kong University and had many good things to say about China."

"Of course I remember." Keng Erh smiled. He too had seen the news item, and he even recalled the subject of her speech: "How I Came to Know China." Indeed, how could he have forgotten Han Suyin, even though he had never talked to anyone else about seeing her.

Early in the summer of 1973 he had gone to Kwangsi province on a geological inspection, and when his work was done, the young colleague who had accompanied him suggested that they stay over for a couple of days so that the young man could visit his parents. Keng Erh was glad to accommodate him, and arranged to wait for him in nearby Kweilin. Keng Erh immediately went to see Hsiao Kin, who was overjoyed to see him. He met her parents, and then he and Hsiao Kin discussed how to spend their windfall of two days together. They decided to take the spectacular river trip from Kweilin to Yangso, so early the next day they lined up at the pier to buy tickets and were fortunate enough to be able to crowd onto one of the boats. Once through the mountain pass and onto the Li River, they were entranced by the magnificent scenery on both shores. Keng Erh had traveled to nearly every spot in North America and had seen many natural wonders, but never had he been so moved.

The clear water of the Li River, the white clouds, the blue sky, and the mountain peaks reflected in the water were like another world. Suddenly Hsiao Kin nudged him, bringing him back to reality. Another boat, less than a hundred meters away, was rapidly coming upon them. A man and a woman were seated in the prow: the man dark-skinned and with a high nose, looking somewhat Indian; the woman obviously part Asian. There was a ring of people, all dressed like mid-level cadre members, standing around this foreign couple, and a fancy tea service, including watermelon and other snacks, was laid out on the table before them.

The woman's face looked familiar to Keng Erh. "Ah, that's right," he said softly to Hsiao Kin, suddenly recognizing her. "That's Han Suyin. I've seen her in the movies and on television."

"Oh, really?" Hsiao Kin's eyes grew wide and her eyebrows arched as she stared at the foreign tourists. "There was a newspaper article about Comrade Chiang Ch'ing meeting her. If that's the case, then that fellow who looks like an Indian must be her husband. I thought that since his name was Lu, he must be a Chinese."

Han Suyin and her husband were pointing at the scenic wonders around them, and delight was written on their faces. Their boat soon passed the tour boat, and Keng Erh quickly put them out of his mind. He was aware only of the magnificent scenery and Hsiao Kin's description of the lovely sights they were passing: Ginkgo Nut Sandbar, Lady in the Mirror . . .

A stirring among the other passengers roused him. The special boat was lying dead in the water directly ahead of them. The glamorous Han Suyin could be seen, talking and laughing animatedly.

"What's going on, comrade?" he asked the person next to him.

"It looks like the motor on the foreign tourists' boat has broken down, and our captain is going over to help them fix it."

"We're going to be late getting to Yangso," another passenger said anxiously, as he looked at his wristwatch.

The motor on the special boat was soon running again,

and it continued on its way. As the distance between the two
boats lengthened rapidly, it was obvious that the regular tour
boat was not moving at all! The passengers were then informed that their trip was cancelled because the motor had
been removed and placed in the foreign visitors' boat. Keng
Erh still remembered the disappointment and anger on the
faces of the tourists.

"That sort of thing happens all the time," Mrs. Chang
commented indifferently, after hearing Keng Erh's story.

"The problem was that most of the people on our boat
were travelers in a hurry to get somewhere."

Hsiao Chang shook his head at Keng Erh's stubbornness.
"Have you forgotten, Lao Keng?" he asked with a smile,
"even though every word Lin Piao ever spoke is now poison,
there is a great deal of truth in what he said at Tienanmen:
'The losses suffered in the Cultural Revolution were very,
very small, while the rewards were very, very great.' Why?
Because political rewards are the most important of all. What
does it matter that twenty or thirty people couldn't get to
Yangso? But it matters a great deal to have Han Suyin say
something good about China abroad."

"But, the problem is . . ."

And yet Keng Erh couldn't say just what the problem
was. He wondered how Han Suyin felt about the incident.

At nine-thirty, after the guests had finished their fruit,
Keng Erh rose and reluctantly said he had to leave. He had
hoped to broach the subject of seeing Hsiao Kin again, but
the opportunity to speak to her had never arisen.

"Lao Keng, come over and see us whenever you've nothing to do," Chang said sincerely. "My wife and I are very

informal. The children, too, look forward to seeing you; they want to study English with you someday."

"I'll come for sure," he said quickly as he patted little Ling-ling's shoulder. He was a little ashamed that he had consciously avoided the family for two whole years.

Hsiao Kin went into the adjoining room to fetch an intricately woven bamboo basket, which she gave to Keng Erh. Inside the basket were a jar of Kweilin spiced fermented bean curd and a bottle of wine. "I didn't bring you anything special, just a couple of local products," she said softly.

"Hsiao Kin . . ." He looked at the basket, then at her, so moved for the moment that he did not know how to express his gratitude. The little bit of wine she had drunk had brought a pinkness to her cheeks and a sparkle to her eyes. The tiny wrinkles around her eyes heightened the expressiveness of her features, so that her smile held even greater charm. As for Keng Erh, the wine and an evening of happiness had brought a warmth to his body and a lightness to his feet. At that very moment he made up his mind to send in another marriage request. This time he would write a letter to Premier Chou and if necessary get his old classmate from America to help. Upon his return from the assignment in Kwangsi he had planned to pursue the matter seriously, but unfortunately the Anti-Lin Piao, Anti-Confucius campaign had been mounted, and he had no choice but to let the matter lie. He now rebuked himself for having moved so slowly.

"I'll see you out to the main gate," Hsiao Kin said as she picked up her cap and gloves.

Hsiao Chang had already put on his cap and coat, but he

quickly took off his cap. "Well, then, I won't be seeing you out. Lao Keng, be sure to come over when you have the time."

Although it was below freezing, with Hsiao Kin beside him Keng Erh didn't feel the cold. His heart seemed to be beating in rhythm with the little bamboo basket swaying from the handlebars of his bicycle. The distant sound of firecrackers accentuated the stillness of this New Year's eve.

Keng Erh had grown accustomed to silence and loneliness, but only at that moment, as he walked beside Hsiao Kin, gently resting his hand on her shoulder, was he finally able to savor the peace and security that are born of silence. In this rare mood of happiness, he had even less desire to speak, and Hsiao Kin, too, conscious of her own feelings, remained quiet so as not to shatter this peaceful moment.

When they reached the street beyond the West Gate, Hsiao Kin finally broke the silence. "Lao Keng," she said in a weak and hesitant voice, as she slowed her pace.

"Hm?"

He looked down affectionately at her and gently pulled her closer to him.

"I . . ." She started to speak, but she stopped with a frightened look in her eyes, as though she were searching for something, or making an appeal, or even performing an act of penance.

"What's wrong, Hsiao Kin?" Keng Erh came to a halt, bent over slightly, and looked at her anxiously.

She turned away abruptly. Then with great difficulty she managed to speak the words "I'm married."

"Married?" he echoed. The hand he had placed on her

shoulder fell limply to his side.

She quickly turned around and looked up at him.

"You're angry," she said, frowning. "You think I wasn't willing to wait. But I had no choice!" Her voice was mournful, but it also carried a note of protest.

"It's all my fault," Keng Erh said at last, feeling utterly spent.

"Don't talk like that." Seeing how dejected he was, Hsiao Kin felt even worse, but she tried to smooth things over by saying gently, "My background is no good, and to have gone on waiting would have been harmful to you."

Keng Erh sensed that his tone had been too harsh, and felt that he had let her down badly. How could she have waited any longer? He reproached himself bitterly. I never gave her enough hope—I was too selfish.

He was suddenly aware of the bone-chilling cold. He started to move again, supporting Hsiao Kin with one hand and pushing his bicycle along with the other.

"I'm glad you got married, Hsiao Kin." He forced himself to be calm and was proud of his self-control. "What you've done is absolutely right, and I wish you happiness."

Hsiao Kin walked with her head down, not making a sound.

"Your husband . . . where is he now?" Keng Erh tried to sound casual, but the word "husband" stuck in his throat. "Just look, I may have lost a prospective wife, but I've gained a friend."

Hsiao Kin looked at him gratefully. "He's an old cadreman. He's been an invalid for more than ten years. His two children work in the Northeast and they both have their own families, so he doesn't care at all if people criticize him about his second marriage. The authorities knew that he needed someone to take care of him in his old age, and naturally they won't be sending me out into the countryside."

Poor woman! Keng Erh loved her more at this moment than ever before.

"Why didn't he come along with you to Peking?" he asked. "Sometimes a change of scene is good for a sick person."

"He'll be here tomorrow," she said weakly.

Tomorrow! Keng Erh was so completely taken by surprise that his heel nearly got caught in the rear wheel of his bicycle. Why hadn't they come together? He nearly blurted out the question, but he saw the look of hopelessness and surrender on Hsiao Kin's face.

They walked on in silence.

"Hsiao Kin, you are a brave woman. I'm sure your husband will be good to you. When he gets here, give me a phone call and I'll give him a nice welcome."

"Oh, Lao Keng . . ." She halted abruptly and shook her head. "I don't think we should see each other again."

Not see each other again! The words struck at his heart.

"Lao Keng, I want you to understand." She was almost imploring him. "I couldn't take it; I just know I couldn't take it!"

Hsiao Kin suddenly lost her composure, and tears welled up in her eyes. She didn't bother to wipe them away, but just let them run down her cheeks.

"I won't go any farther with you," she said at last.

Keng Erh grasped her shoulder tightly. "I'll see you

back," he said. But Hsiao Kin shook her head resolutely, wiped the tears from her face, and pulled away from his grasp. She looked up at him once more and said softly, "Goodbye." Her footsteps got faster and faster, and finally she lowered her head and ran into one of the alleys.

For a long time Keng Erh stood looking down the deserted street where she had just walked. From somewhere came the sputter of exploding firecrackers and the gleeful shouts of children. But for Keng Erh, there was only loneliness ahead.

Nixon's Press Corps

THE BUGLE CALLS BLARING FROM THE LOUDSPEAKERS THAT greeted our arrival at school in the morning seemed to be louder and more insistent than usual. Just as we were wondering what it was all about, one of the teachers told us that an emergency meeting of all departments had been called. My husband and I hurried over to the large classroom in which such meetings were usually held. It was already packed with teachers and workers. Lao Ho, the head of the Department Revolutionary Committee, and Lao Tiao, the delegate from the Workers' Publicity Corps, were sitting alone in the front row; Lao Ho was leaning over and listening intently as Lao Tiao, head bent and eyes crinkled, whispered into his ear. As always, my husband and I silently went our separate ways to join colleagues from our own teaching groups.

"Why are we having another general meeting?" I asked a colleague as I sat down.

"I hear it's on account of Nixon's press corps. It seems they're actually coming here," she whispered back.

This news eased my concern. I leaned back in my chair and waited for the meeting to begin. As long as they weren't launching some political campaign or purging someone, I had nothing to worry about. In preparation for Nixon's forthcoming visit, a general study of all pertinent documents had begun three months earlier. The visit had already become a familiar and accepted thing. One would think that after twenty years of attacking "American Imperialism" as the number one enemy, it would be difficult for people to change their way of thinking to such an extent that they would shake hands and fraternize with the President of the United States. But after an intensive reading of all the circulated documents, their thoughts began to fall in line with what they read. No one ever publicly questioned the contradictory statements or this about-face in Communist policy. When it was announced that Nixon's press corps would be passing through Nanking, the provincial and metropolitan commissioners made elaborate preparations for the visit. Even the street committees were given sample questions that the correspondents might ask, so that everyone could practice giving appropriate answers.

The loudspeakers stopped promptly at eight, and we all checked our watches.

Lao Ho was the first to address us. "Good morning, comrades! By direction of the provincial authorities, we have called this meeting to complete preparations for receiving

Nixon's press corps. The eighty-man press group traveling with Nixon may pass through Nanking tomorrow for a one-day visit, so we must be ready. Today we will suspend all normal activities in order to have a general clean-up and to tidy up the lawns. All laboratory equipment must be cleaned and labeled in both Chinese and English; if necessary, get some help from the Foreign Languages Section. We believe that the reporters will be in Nanking for the day only, so the possibility of a visit to our school is very remote. But as Chairman Mao has taught us, 'Do not fight unprepared battles.' Therefore, we will proceed with preparations in order to be ready for any and all contingencies. We will now ask Lao Tiao, Chairman Mao's good worker from the Publicity Corps, to say a few words to us."

Lao Tiao stood up slowly. His small eyes coldly swept over the hall. He cleared his throat loudly and placed one foot on the chair beside Lao Ho. With his right hand on his raised knee and his left hand resting on his hip, he was the very picture of self-assurance and arrogance. Not a sound was to be heard in the classroom, as all eyes were on his raised leg. He reminded me of the villain, Tiao Te-i, in the revolutionary Peking opera *Sha Chia Pang*.

Lao Tiao began with the usual line about the world revolutionary movements signaling the end of the road for American imperialism. Then he said that Nixon had been forced to come begging for peace, and he repeated some of the standard doctrines and policies. Then he reminded everyone: "It is of the utmost importance for us to grasp the characteristics of these reporters. They have their 'three excesses'— an excess of running around, an excess of questions, and an excess of picture taking. But we have our ways of dealing with them: We must maintain an attitude neither overbearing nor humble, neither too approachable nor too distant, neither . . . er, er . . . in other words, if we maintain an attitude of 'three neithers' in dealing with their 'three excesses,' we shall remain invincible."

Suddenly he raised his voice and declared emphatically, "Don't go milling about on the streets tomorrow unless you have something important to do! There are some who must pay special attention to this, who must behave themselves and refrain from any untoward conduct!"

At first I didn't understand what he was talking about. But my face burned when it dawned on me that I might be the object of this veiled warning. I didn't dare look up, for fear that I might meet other people's eyes. I felt so uneasy that I was barely able to sit still. This kind of oblique attack—mentioning no names, but letting one "find one's own seat"—was devastatingly effective. Protesting one's innocence was interpreted as proof of a guilty conscience, so the only thing to do was to swallow the whole thing, no matter how distasteful.

After the general meeting we separated into various discussion groups. While the leader of our group was off receiving his instructions, Hsiao Wei, our news-monger, whose wife had just come from Peking to visit him, took the opportunity to let us in on a bit of gossip. Rumor had it that during Kissinger's second visit, a woman dashed out to accost him with a written complaint as his car was passing along Changan Boulevard. She was immediately hustled off by plainclothesmen and jailed as a counterrevolutionary. The woman's husband was an old Party cadreman who must have been purged during the Cultural Revolution. Evidently she tried to enlist Kissinger's help in bringing up his case for reconsideration.

"She had a lot of nerve but very little sense," Hsiao Wei said. "She should have known that they wouldn't let anyone get close to a foreign visitor, especially Kissinger!"

Although this was only a rumor and there was no indication that the woman had been an overseas Chinese, or a returnee from the United States like me, I played it cautiously anyway. As soon as the discussion began I stood up and declared that, except for going directly to and from the classroom, I would not budge from my home all the next day, not even to go to the market. A rightist in the group also made a similar declaration. Afterwards, as we were cleaning up, our group leader came up and patted my shoulder. "Don't be so touchy, Hsiao Hsin, Lao Tiao didn't necessarily mean you."

My only response was a forced smile.

When we went home at noon, both my husband and I were feeling very depressed. We ate our lunch in silence.

"We won't even be going to the market tomorrow," I said, "so you had better go now before you go back to work. Just pick up anything—a vegetable or two will be enough."

He was somewhat taken aback for a moment, but he nodded, and went out with the market basket. I was too weary and dispirited even to clear the table, so I just sat there in a daze until a knock at the door brought me around.

"Who is it?" I asked as I opened the door. It was Hsiao Miao, a member of our neighborhood committee.

"Hsin Lao-shih, have you finished lunch?"

"Yes, come in." I made way for her. "Is there something on your mind?"

"Yes," she said solemnly, ignoring my invitation. "We've received orders to clean up the courtyard because Nixon's press corps is coming tomorrow. We are to pull up the weeds, remove the litter from all the nooks and crannies, and . . ." Here she hesitated. "We also have to take down all the drying racks over the windows. They're afraid the foreign visitors will find them an eyesore."

"Take down all the drying racks?" Although this struck me as funny to the point of absurdity, I was unable to laugh.

"Hsiao Miao," I said, "with all the famous scenic and historic sites in Nanking, why would the reporters take the time to come to this isolated area during a one-day visit to the city? And if by chance they happened to pass by here, they will be sitting in cars. And even if they were to stand on top of the cars they still could not see through our gate, to this building four rows back. They wouldn't even be able to see the roof, let alone the windows!"

"I'm just acting on orders from the neighborhood committee." She sighed, spreading her hands in a gesture of helplessness. "I have to take mine down even though it was put up only last month."

I couldn't encourage her to refuse to tear hers down, but I shook my head to express my opposition. We had gone through a lot of trouble to put up our rack two years before. My husband went all the way to the old Confucius Temple area to buy the bamboo poles, and since wire was not available in the markets, I begged a colleague to get me a small roll of it from his laboratory. Then my husband and I spent almost an entire day putting up a rack with three cross pieces outside our south window. It was sturdily built and strong enough to sun a pair of quilts. But two years of wind and rain had already rusted the wires, and if we tore the rack down now we would never be able to put it up again.

"I can't take ours down," I declared stubbornly. "You have my word that I won't hang any clothes out tomorrow, but I simply can't take it down. If I did I wouldn't be able to put it up again. Where would I hang our clothes to dry then? After all, Nixon's reporters are people too. It's unlikely they would say anything when they saw the racks. And if they did, we could take the opportunity to 'reeducate' them and teach them a thing or two!"

Hsiao Miao had no answer to that. She just looked distressed and waved her hands. "All right, but don't say I didn't notify you."

That afternoon as I walked through the dormitory gate on my way home from work I saw all the elderly people cleaning up the yard. Some were raking leaves, others were removing dead grass. Because of the cold, they were so bundled up in heavy clothing that their movements appeared even slower and clumsier than usual. The drying racks for the first row of houses facing the road had all vanished. As I walked farther in I saw that most of the racks in the next row had already been taken down, and the rest were being dismantled. The people were working in sullen silence. I was relieved to see that our rack was still safe and untouched, although those around it were gone. One neighbor was just removing the last piece of wood from his rack; he broke it off with a resounding crack and threw the pieces to the ground without a glance. Our rack stood out in lonely splendor in the deepening dusk. I didn't know whether to feel proud or apprehensive.

My husband and son came home before long. As soon as he entered the door my husband cried, "This is sheer madness—a single word and everyone is dismantling them! Just now someone asked me, 'Are you really going to leave yours up?' I could barely keep from asking him, 'Why are you tearing yours down? If we all refused, what could they do about it?"

"That's enough," I interrupted, glancing at the child.

He immediately dropped the subject.

"Be a good boy and go play in the other room. Mommy will call you as soon as dinner is ready."

With the child out of the way, my husband followed me into the kitchen and demanded, "How about it? Do we tear ours down or not?"

"Of course we don't!" I declared indignantly. "Just because of Nixon's visit, they want us to slap our own faces! The whole country has been frantic for almost three months, and, now, just because some members of his press corps might pass through here for a day, we're supposed to turn the place upside down for them. We're not even free to go out on the streets! What makes them think I'd want to see the reporters anyway? I'm not even interested in Nixon himself! I still remember his disgraceful performance on television in the midst of the 1952 presidential campaign. He dragged in his dog, Checkers, to get sympathy for his defense against bribery charges. My American roommate was so disgusted that she called him 'political garbage!' Since we're never trusted and we can't afford to protest, we can let an inanimate object like our drying rack stand up for us. The most they can do is tear it to pieces."

My husband tried to soothe me, "All right, all right, we won't tear it down. Just don't make yourself ill. Get dinner ready while I clean up the yard."

We had made our decision, yet I was so distracted I couldn't cook properly. The rice was burned, and the spinach was still raw. Neither of us had any appetite, and we couldn't find anything to talk about, so we hurried through the meal in silence. Only our son, in his innocence, was his usual self, eating heartily and chattering away.

I had just cleared the table and was about to pour some water to bathe the boy's feet, when my husband rushed in from the other room in great agitation.

"Kao Sao is coming this way, probably to our house. I can't bear that woman, so you'd better talk to her. If she's here about the drying rack, don't argue with her; just take it down!"

I grew uneasy at the mention of Kao Sao's name. It had never occurred to me that this affair would warrant a personal visit from the chairwoman of the neighborhood committee of our dormitory area. She came from a good background— before Liberation her family had been impoverished, I was told—and her husband was a laborer and a Party member. Ever since the founding of the school she and her whole family lived in our dormitory gatehouse, and she was given the responsibility of delivering messages. Though she was still under forty, she was very experienced and capable, especially in handling purges within the dormitory. When she attacked the women, the old, and the weak she was truly awesome. Because of her good background, she had felt free to bear six children, one after the other, but since her husband's wages were insufficient to support them all, they relied on welfare from the state to get by. No shining example of planned parenthood herself, she was nonetheless a staunch supporter of birth control and an eloquent advocate of abortion. She had had little education, but she had been born with a glib tongue, and with her high-pitched voice and caustic remarks, no woman was her match. Mao Tse-tung has said that women hold up half the sky, and it seemed to me that in the corner of earth where our dormitory was located, Kao Sao held it up single-handedly.

"Stay here and don't come out," I said as I pushed my husband back into the room. I hurriedly wiped my hands, put my son's shoes back on his feet, and scooted him into the other room. Just as I shut the door behind me, there was a knock on the front door.

Sure enough, there stood Kao Sao.

"Hsin Lao-shih, have you already had dinner?"

Her words were polite, but her face was cold and unsmiling. With her hands held behind her back, she looked me over from head to foot to show that she meant business and was not to be trifled with.

"Yes, I have!" I answered. My heart was thumping wildly, and I could hear my own breathing, but I remained standing in the doorway, unwilling to give way.

"Are you here because of the drying rack?" I decided to come right to the point.

"That's right. Yours is the only one left in the entire

dormitory, and if it's not taken down you'll be putting us in an awkward position with the authorities."

Naturally, I repeated the reasons I had given Hsiao Miao that morning. But Kao Sao proved a formidable opponent. She said nothing about the possibility of the reporters' passing along our road, but stressed instead the importance of discipline within the revolutionary ranks. She even quoted many of Mao Tse-tung's sayings, so that in the end, my refusal to dismantle the rack became a political issue. Political pressure is too heavy a burden to accept lightly, and so my anger mounted as I listened to the harangue. Curiously enough, the overall effect was to quiet me down.

Finally, I said calmly, "I don't think you should make so much of this. After all, it's only a small matter, and my refusal to tear the thing down isn't unreasonable. In discussing any issue, one must begin with the major premise, which in the present case is that we should put our best foot forward for our foreign guests. There is no problem here, because I am in complete agreement with the premise. The question is this: What is wrong with drying racks? Even in America there are still many people who hang their clothes out to dry in their backyards . . ."

"I don't know what they do in America, and I don't care!" she interrupted me with a wave of her hand. "This is China, and we do things the Chinese way."

This argument shamed and distressed me. I stared at her and my cheeks burned as I listened to her high-pitched shouts. The neighbor opposite us gingerly opened her door a crack and stuck her head out, but she quickly closed the door when she saw Kao Sao.

"Nobody knows whether the foreign visitors will pass by here or not, but even if they don't, tearing down a drying rack is at most a small sacrifice for the revolution."

"The state does not advocate unnecessary sacrifices!"

Compared to her strident voice, the tone of my protest was low and my voice was small, shaky, and very weak.

"If the foreign visitors do come through and you're the only family whose drying rack is still standing, we in the Party cadre will have to bear the onus of your refusal to carry out our orders. And even if they don't come, what will the other people say? 'Hsin Lao-shih was right in refusing to tear it down!' It will make it difficult for us to carry on in this area in the future."

I felt like shouting that she was being selfish and thinking only of herself. But she was no one to tangle with. I restrained myself with such force that I trembled all over. There was a sudden pain in my chest, and I couldn't breathe. I pressed my hand against my chest, and, remembering my husband's admonition, decided to give up the argument. I could never get the upper hand with her.

"I'm not going to tear it down," I told her. "If you want it torn down, do it yourself. And you can be responsible for putting it back up when the foreign visitors have gone!"

She was stunned.

"How can I take it down for you?" She quickly changed her tune. "To welcome foreign visitors and clean up the environment is a voluntary action by the revolutionary masses; the Party would never force it on anyone. If you don't tear it down, then the onus is on you, and if anything happens, don't say that we didn't try to carry out our responsibility!"

I hadn't the strength to answer. I just stared at her inverted triangle of a face, which seemed to be growing longer and sharper; her eyes were as arrogant and cold as Lao Tiao's.

"Then that's that!" She spat out the words and walked away with her arms behind her back, her head held high. The hard nylon soles of her cloth shoes tapped a sharp tattoo on the cement outside. I shut the door.

That night I didn't sleep well. I woke with a start several times.

The next day passed quietly and uneventfully. On the third day we heard that Nixon's press corps had shown no interest in Nanking and had gone directly to Hangchow. Two French reporters were the only ones who stopped over, and they had merely strolled around New Market Square before joining the others the same night. And so the people in our dormitory began to pound and nail, as family after family slowly put up its rack again. Long after Nixon left China and arrived back in the United States, the drying racks in our dormitory had still not been completely rebuilt.